# THE ARBITER OF GRAVITY

## THE APPARATUS OF UNITY

YUVRAJ ARORA

# Contents

# Contents

# Prologue

Eons ago, the Primordial Chaos reigned. A storm of entropy, where nothing and everything was one. From this, the Apparatus of Unity was forged, a construct of unimaginable power – the ability to unify Gravity with the other three fundamental forces – Electromagnetism, the Strong Nuclear Force, and the Weak Nuclear Force.

For a while, there was peace, but peace? It is a fragile thing.

Ambition arose, and with it, war. This ambition tore the universe apart.

In this tear of the universe, three great Empires were the most feared:

The Sosush Empire – Wielders of Quantum Mechanics

The Yazoto Foundation – Masters of Plasma

The Trisazal Dominion – Harbingers of Dark Energy

Each Empire was as strong as the other, and their ideologies differed but not their goal. The Apparatus of Unity was the ultimate prize, an object too dangerous to wield but too powerful to ignore.

The creators present in the dormant Primordial Chaos saw this greed for power and, in a desperate attempt, dismantled the Apparatus into three Instruments of Unity and scattered them across the Universe.

She was there. A girl – small, silent, simple, yet mysterious, saw it all. She witnessed the rise and the fall of tension in the universe, from a war for the search for ultimate power to an uneasy silence.

Now, eons later, she watches again.

The Instruments now stir, waiting to be freed, sending signals across the Universe, making every Empire feel the call yet again, unlocking their greed for power. Their fleets burn through spacetime once more.

In this chaos, the girl's gaze falls on one small point in the vast universe – a boy.

A boy, drenched in sweat, lost in dreams with echoes of the Apparatus. A boy unaware of the power he wields, a power tethering him to the scattered Apparatus.

To the girl, he is more than a boy. He is the herald of balance. The Arbiter of Gravity.

The race has begun.

The cosmos holds its breath.

# CHAPTER I

# Oh, my lovely sweaty dreams.

They say dreams are just a way of processing the junk in one's brain, but for me, they've always been different, or should I say *it's* been different. My recurring dream had always been linked to reality, invoking a sense of déjà vu whenever something crazy happened in my life, and this recurring dream started bleeding into reality, slowly but surely, back when I was nine.

It began as a usual dream of mine – getting attacked by a bunch of wild pracos.

Pracos, if you don't know, are huge brown creatures with three legs, a smell so obscene it could even make my smelly friend Daqpo vomit, five multi-coloured eyes, hair longer than my mum's, a small, disfigured nose, crooked lips, and seven arms which each probably weighed 100 Newtons.

As always, I barely escaped them and found myself stumbling on my feet as I saw a person with a presence stronger than a solar wave. This person was a recurring character in my dreams, and I didn't even know who she was.

Her hair was dark and wavy, absorbing the light from the Stars above and shining brighter than them. Her eyes were...yeah, I can't describe them. They were just...different. Her gaze was scary, scary in the sense that

I couldn't look away once I saw it, it was almost magnetic, no short of breathtaking. While, yes, it did distract me, it somehow gave me this weird feeling, a feeling of reassurance, a feeling that I wasn't alone. She always used to wear a weird, yet beautiful, white gown etched with random triangular symbols and sand-coloured sandals, which managed to camouflage with her skin.

She was like the calm in a storm, the only normal thing amongst the chaotic shrieks of the pracos.              Even though I didn't know her and had only ever seen her in my dreams, she felt like stability in a world which constantly shifted beneath my feet.

She never spoke. She was just there, standing, smiling, with an aural radius bigger than that of a supernova. Shockingly, unlike real life, when she was there, I didn't sweat like a maniac in front of a woman.

Yet, as always, before I could even say a word, a praco came and punched me.

Usually, this is the time when I would wake up with a 'hot' sweat. Yes, a 'hot' sweat. Normal people wake up with 'cold' sweats when these events take place, but me? I wake up with hot ones, and no one knows why. My grandma always called me 'special', so I guess it makes sense.

But this time, instead of waking up, I got transported to this dark void. The transportation was seamless; it genuinely felt like it was part of the dream, but somewhere deep down inside of me, I knew it wasn't. I knew it was something else. I couldn't see a thing; everything was pitch black. All I could hear was the hum of a powerful star, the smell of ancient metal I last smelt in my history lesson at school, and the voices of people arguing in a language I couldn't quite understand. They sounded like screeching metal. I think it was two females and one male. Obviously, I was 9 years old, so I tried shouting, but I couldn't. My mouth just couldn't open; it was sealed shut. I was scared for my life.

The arguing continued, and I felt the voices coming nearer. I started sweating even more. See, sweating for me is normal, but this was weird. I could feel myself getting wet everywhere, and no, it wasn't because I peed myself – which I did – because that was only there in my lower body.

Anyhoo, the voices inched closer. I sweated more. The sounds of metal screeching were growing ever so loudly, and this kept happening for about 10 minutes until one of the voices FINALLY spoke in English.

They all spoke four mysterious lines in classic patriarchal fashion; the guy spoke the first two, and the women spoke one each. They said:

> *"To unify the universe and bind the deep,*
> *To end all entropy or make the cosmos go to sleep,*
> *Three artefacts, women of darkness,*
> *Three factions, and a power to harness."*

If I could speak and wasn't terrified for my life, I'd probably say, "Whaaaaaaaaat?" because that was the most confusing thing I'd ever heard, like, what in the world's 'entropy'? What do you mean by 'women of darkness'?

How the heck can the cosmos go to sleep? It literally made no sense to nine-year-old me, and then, to exponentiate the confusion, I could feel something, or someone, softly touch my forehead. I couldn't believe a touch so delicate could bring forth an impact so violent – I flopped around like a fish, and my insides felt like they were being stabbed by multiple tiny needles. I went up and down in the void, and my body felt as if it was about to be pulled apart in half.

Everything hurt, and right at that moment, I felt one last downward push and found myself back in my bed.

I woke up, unsurprisingly, with a bucketful of hot sweat and my lower wet...for obvious reasons.

Then, like a little baby, I went to my parents and cried – yeah, with the wet clothes.

Now, even seven years later, at the ripe age of sixteen, those words still confuse me. What did those three people, if they were people, mean? Like, sure, okay, I know what entropy means now – Chaos – but those other questions are still there in my brain.

I also got to know one more thing: the girl's name.

Seren.

Her name was just the cherry on top of her otherworldly appearance. I first started hearing it around a year before, back when I was 15, always in the segment of my recurring dream when I saw her. The sound of her name felt like a direct whisper from the cosmos. It was just special. Even though it shouldn't have taken me a while, I managed to finally connect the random 'Sssss-eren' sound to the beautiful lady only around a few days ago as the sound started getting louder. I think I somehow managed to annoy the cosmos. I really am amazing.

Anyway, even though I was happy that I had all this information, it did come with a weird price – zoning out, even in important situations, such as this one morning during my holidays – the sky was crimson red, as it always is in my home-planet of Keo III, with fully black clouds and stars that never really stand out because it's always dark.

The morning was mostly normal, except there was this…I don't know, weird sound, a hum of sorts, like a monk meditating but also not really. It pierced through my body, vibrated my bones and made me feel uneasy. The level of uneasiness was similar to that of the dream, which wasn't really a dream, so something inside me told me that they were connected. There was also this smell…it was a smell I'd smelt before, but I couldn't quite place it.

My smelly friend Daqpo knew something was off as well, and no, the smell wasn't his disgusting body odour. I'm immune to it at this point.

See, Daqpo, whilst extremely smelly, was like a brother to me. We'd known each other since pre-school and have had each other's back ever since. His appearance was completely opposite to mine, which I think made our bond stronger. Contrary to my relatively light skin, five feet eleven-inch height, straight black hair, brown eyes, he had dark skin, was barely as tall as an average nine-year-old, salt-and-pepper hair as if he was a grandpa, and had pitch black eyes. He accompanied me in basically everything I ever did – except, like, taking a shower or something.

At that moment, he was scratching his head.

"You hear that?" he asked, breaking the silence.

"Hear what?"

"Can't you hear it? The sounds of metal screeching? A sound similar to what we heard...that day?"

I froze at his words.

The mention of *that day* just had this weird effect. It always sent shivers down my entire body. It wasn't something that we didn't want to talk about. We just couldn't. It was...eh, I really can't describe it with any words except *weird*.

"Yeah," I said. My voice barely came out of my throat because the only thing I felt was weakness. *That day* just...ugh.

Daqpo tensed, "The vibes are all the same, remember when we-?"

"Yeah, no, I got you," I said, cutting him off. I knew everything was the same, but I didn't want him to mention it.

See, *that day* started off as a completely mundane Tuesday. Daqpo and I were on our way to our usual scavenging spot – the Fields of Srizure – fields that were once a thriving harvesting spot back when my parents were kids, back when they were just called 'The Fields'. But stuff changed after the Second Galactic War between the Sosush Empire and Nunoki Dynasty. After the fields were completely destroyed during the conflict, they were renamed in honour of Emperor Srizure, the ruler of the planet's galactic system at the time, who led the Sosush to victory. Funny how a third-grade history lesson, which I thought I paid no attention to, just came flooding back, but yeah, where was I? The Fields of Srizure weren't exactly the safest spot to go to for scavenging. The terrain had been messy since the war, and it was easy to trip or lose your breath because of all the weird fumes that were around, but Daqpo and I were experienced enough not to fall for any of that.

We wore masks and our brown scavenging overalls, and I had this random walking stick I'd found lying around in my house to check for any crevices as I led the way.

To be honest, we found a pretty mid-haul – some spare engine parts, but that's when I saw this little sparkling thing under some dusty old rocks.

It was shiny, black, and had a rectangular pattern on it. It seemed mysterious, so I did what anyone would do: call their best friend.

"DAQPOOOOOOOOOOO," I yelled, "Yo, come here for a sec."

Daqpo came running, and as soon as he saw it, he said, "Dude, put that in your bag *right now*."

"What the heck? What if it's something dangerous?"

"What if it's something dangerous?" he mocked me, "Our last few hauls have been *useless*, Yelix. We've reached a stage where it's either scavenge something crazy or starve, and I *don't* want our parents to starve. Put it in the bag before I do."

I sighed, "Okay."

I went over to grab it, my body trembling. Just as I touched the thing, I was back in the void. Yes, the void I was in in the not-a-dream-dream.

Instead of hearing people indistinctly arguing in a language I couldn't really understand, I saw her. Seren.

She was in the same indescribable outfit and had the same infectious aura as before, but this time, she spoke.

Her voice was...yeah, no. I'd rather not describe it.

She said, "The First. You've found it," and then she disappeared, but I was still in the void.

For about five seconds, I thought I'd died, but then something appeared in front of me – a map. A map of stars, with a few stars brighter than the others. I was on one of the brighter stars. It meant something. I didn't quite know what, but it definitely meant *something*. But, before I could make any sense of it, it disappeared right in front of my eyes, and Seren came back.

"Keep this with you, for the women of darkness approach. Go northward, find the unraveller of entropy."

Now, she disappeared. Her tone this time seemed tense as if she was urging me to go northward IMMEDIATELY.

Then, I felt something similar to what I felt the last time I was in the void and then landed back in the fields and woke up to find Daqpo completely pale, shaking me as if I was dead. Ideally, I should've started my journey to the 'unraveller of entropy' right at that moment, but I was too scared. Instead, I continued scavenging for more stuff because, well, money over life, right? I mean, I'm something of an expert at defying people, so I ignored her urgency with ease.

Since then, everything's been crazy. A dream I had seven years ago was suddenly turning into reality, and I really didn't know what to do, and neither did Daqpo. Unknown people in strange suits had started coming over to ask questions which neither my family nor I could comprehend. The thing which we found – the shiny rock, or 'The First' – sparkled brighter on some nights than others, and, to top it all, I could SWEAR it also spoke to me sometimes.

And now, when we felt the same vibes as *that day*, I knew it wasn't over. I knew something was about to happen.

And it did. Out of the crimson-red haze of the Fields of Srizure, they came. It was an ambush.

# CHAPTER II

# What the heck have I gotten myself into?

Honestly? I regret ignoring Seren's urgency.

Three giant figures came out of the haze like shadows given form, each of them about two feet taller than me, wearing the same attire – a suit, a facemask, and a sword, all in the same color – black – with the same glowing random parabolic patterns on them. If their size wasn't already terrifying, each step that they took left a small crater beneath them in the already hilly ground. Each step they took sounded like a hammer hitting a metal sheet, then scratching past it. I don't know about the smelly guy next to me, but I was scared for my life.

As if on cue, we both started running at the same time and smacked into each other. Great job, you smelly pepper melon Daq.

As we picked ourselves up, the next thing I knew, they had surrounded us in a triangular shape, keeping their distance as if they were playing with us.

Daqpo and I were back-to-back. Either there was a massive quake, or Daqpo was shivering like crazy. Probably a mixture of both because, as the three figures prepared to pounce on us like predators, I'm pretty sure they moved a few tectonic plates as well.

They inched closer in the same triangular formation, and as if I'd woken up from a dream, I was dripping with sweat, and if it went on any longer, my odour would've probably gotten worse than Daqpo.

But that's when the first one spoke, "Pow pow... empo likey..."

I couldn't quite understand what he said, but I do know that he sounded like metal slime. And, to top it all off, he spoke softer and slower than my fifth-grade math teacher. Like, how can you look so menacing yet sound so dumb?

Then, as they continuously edged closer, another one spoke, "Wataka."

Now, see, this one really creeped me out because (1) he sounded like an assassin, (2) he glowed when he said whatever he said, so that probably was a boost of energy, and (3) he sounded weirdly confident. I was quite sure that he was the leader of the trinity of predators.

I was wrong.

The third one made a noise, and oh boy, my river of sweat turned into a waterfall. This one just grunted, and his grunt exerted a force so big that I'm pretty sure that it destabilized me a bit. *He* was the leader, not the previous one.

They slowly continued moving closer.

I was trying to look intimidating by holding the stick in my hand, but it didn't really work. They didn't stop.

Something inside of me felt like they were behind the shiny rock thingie we came in possession of, so I positioned myself in a way where my bag was between Daqpo and me.

They pounced.

The one I presumed to be the leader made one final grunt, and they all jumped back into the crimson-red haze for a microsecond before they came out, headfirst with their swords in their hand – the sharp side pointing straight at me.

The leader was about two inches away from me, and that's when it happened.

By it, I mean the weirdest moment of my entire lifetime, one drop of sweat passed over my forehead, onto my left eyebrow and landed straight on that stick I was holding.

As soon as the drop of hot sweat and stick made contact, an extremely powerful outwards force was exerted, like a shockwave. It pushed all the predators away and somehow kept Daqpo safe as if the stick had a mind of its own, somehow knowing that Daqpo was a smelly yet friendly person. To top it all off, it didn't make a sound. It *absorbed* sound. The terrain moved up and down as if gravity itself decided to throw a tantrum.

But that's when stuff got even more weird.

The stick started to vibrate and glow as if it were alive. It wasn't just shining; it felt like it was pulling light towards it, bending reality. I really wanted to let go, but I just...I just couldn't. It was like the stick was holding onto me.

Then it dissolved. Its edges became blurry, and slowly, it went from opaque to translucent to transparent. It was gone, but that's when I felt it, not in my hand, but in *me*.

It felt like liquid light coursing through my veins. It wasn't unpleasant; it was activating. For a moment, all the nerves in my body lit up, and the area around me turned...curvy. Like it was distorted as if I pulled part of it. I could feel the stick threading through me, becoming one with me. My whole body hummed with energy.

But then it stopped.

I stared at my hand, expecting it to fall off or some weird runes to show up like they do in the fantasy movies I'd watched, but nothing like that happened. No mutations either. I *looked* completely normal when, in actuality, I wasn't. The stick wasn't gone. It had gone *in*.

Daqpo was just sitting there, staring at me with awe, "Dude."

"What?" I asked.

"*Dude*," he said again.

"*What*," I asked, irritated.

"Did you just *see* what happened? *So* cool!" he exclaimed.

Honestly, I didn't have an answer because I still couldn't understand what happened, so I just said, "Eh."

"What's wro—"

The grunting guy interrupted him by laughing maniacally and then proceeding to speak for the first time ever, "Empo...de oa al...de...pow"

He sounded scary. He looked scary. But holy biology was his language stupid (sidenote – biology, for my planet, is the family-friendly equivalent for the s word). I couldn't help but laugh.

I think my laughing kind of pissed him off. He charged. He pushed Daqpo aside as he came towards me. I wanted to run, but that energetic feeling inside of me stopped me. He raised his sword, ready to strike.

I instinctively closed my eyes and clenched my fists.

There it was: the same energy from the stick, or whatever it was I felt before. It surged through me. But whatever I was trying to do backfired *hard*.

One moment, I was weightless. The other, I was on the ground, then weightless again. It definitely wasn't as graceful and cool as I thought it'd be. I endlessly bounced up and down to the point where Daqpo wasn't scared anymore and started laughing like a maniac.

I couldn't see it quite clearly, but the predator's head also tilted in confusion.

He tried to strike me mid-air, but his sword froze just before it could hit me. It seemed like it hit an invisible barrier. It vibrated more violently than the ground when the predators stepped on it, with the patterns shifting away from me, glowing brighter than before. The air around us warped in a way similar to how it did when the stick fused inside of me. *Space* wasn't letting the sword through.

The patterns on the predator shone brighter. He tried again, but, unlucky for him, the same phenomena took place, except this time, instead of the sword being flung back, it slid over the invisible barrier. The air warped again, but a spark of purple flame ignited this time for a brief moment.

Daqpo gasped, "Yo, it's like his glowy sword is hitting an invisible barrier!"

"Thanks for speaking the obvious, Daq," I muttered whilst still being flung up and down endlessly.

The predator grunted again. With my blurry vision, I could see his sword change shape as if it were alive. It hummed louder than it was before whilst it was altering its shape. Simultaneously, the predator circled around me, looking for different angles to attack me from.

Honestly, I didn't know what was happening, but I had a brief idea. The stick's fusion with me led to the formation of some kind of invisible barrier around me, and I think the predator should've known that by then as well, but he didn't. He grunted and then lunged at my feet with his sword, now looking like an axe.

Bad move.

As soon as he swung his axe, the same purple spark arose. But this time, the spark got transferred over to the axe, and it started to contract, it was like it was getting sucked into itself. Its shininess kept increasing, till the point where it almost got blinding, and then *SCHUP*! It broke, evaporating into the air like ashes. That *SCHUP.* caused a shockwave big enough to push the predator back, making him fall on his back on the rocky terrain.

At the same time, I hit the ground with a thud as gravity, or whatever it was, stopped messing with me. I looked over at the now-fallen predator, his patterns coming back to the brightness they were at before this entire battle or whatever started.

He seemed tired, but he still managed to speak, "Pow...bi pow...Harjan za Zecond likey..."

"'Harjan za Zecond', is that your name?" I asked, trying to get that question in before he started retreating or attacking me again, with my voice barely making its way out of my throat.

He grunted, got up, and left.

'Cold attitude, man', I thought to myself.

Behind him, the other two, who just watched our battle, got up and followed him.

Daqpo came running to me, "Yelix! Are you okay?"

"Yeah, man, thanks."

He picked me up, "What *was* that?"

"I don't know, but it's like, it's like there's this *thing* inside of me."

"Huh?"

Right that moment, the slimy voice predator came out of the haze again, said, "La zhozu wi co...be re i," and then went back.

Daqpo and I both tilted our heads, but then it struck me.

Seren's words: "Go northward, find the unraveller of entropy."

I immediately turned my head towards Daqpo and said, "We need to go north."

It's time I finally did what Seren asked me to before things got any worse. Maybe I can get some answers for what happened to me, or who these people are, or what 'The First' is.

# CHAPTER III

# Who knew convincing my parents was going to be the most difficult part of the journey?

You'd think convincing my parents after nearly dying would be an easy job. Spoiler alert: it wasn't. Somehow, nearly getting skewered by stupid language-strong appearance predators isn't a valid argument for freedom.

So, we got back to town safe and sound. I told *everything* that happened to Daqpo on the way back, and somehow, he just found everything cool and not disturbing at all. Math bless his dumb soul (another sidenote – Math is the equivalent of what religious people call 'God' in my galactic system).

On our way back, to make stuff easier for us, we came up with what we *thought* would be a foolproof plan:

1.  convince Daqpo's parents (easy, they barely care),
2.  convince my parents (very tough, they care too much),
3.  get our friend Kanzon to join us because he's got the brains that the two of us lack (he's an orphan, so that rules out convincing his parents),
4.  use one of the spare travel pods that Kanzon has created (and pray to Math that it doesn't explode), and
5.  use my *literal* mind map to head to the 'Unraveller of Entropy' (whatever that means).

What could go wrong?

Everything went wrong except, well, the first step. Step 1 was pretty simple. We didn't even have to say much before Daqpo's parents said yes. I guess keeping an eye on the Sosush Empire's political state as Senators leaves little time for helicopter parenting. Fine by us.

Step 1 went off without a hitch, but, as always, the universe *had* to balance it by making Step 2 an absolute nightmare.

My parents were very protective of me. I didn't mind it until, well, now, when I really, *really* needed to go out. I kept pleading with them, but they wouldn't budge.

Mum was like, "Yelix, look at yourself. All your clothes are torn up. Do you really expect us to send you away, possibly *closer* to more danger, just because you had a vision?"

My mom was wearing a yellow dress, with her pink heels. She had some makeup covering her face – there was some mascara covering her brown eyes, some blush all over her narrow nose and cheeks, with red lipstick and some weird powder on her short brown hair. She was as tall as my chest.

Dad was a bit fifty-fifty. He wanted me to go out on my own, but he was scared about me dying, so he was just there, nodding his head and saying stuff like 'mhm', 'hm', 'ah!', et cetera. Basic dad stuff.

Dad was wearing simple clothes: a formal red shirt, black trousers, and black shoes. His black hair was slicked back and his red eyes and black beard looked scary yet calming as usual, his six foot three inches height towering over me.

They were definitely planning to go on a date that day, but I think I ruined their plans. I didn't care to ask else Mom might've given me another lecture on top of the one I was already getting.

I literally even said the most dramatic paragraph of my *life*, something which, honestly, I couldn't believe was coming out of my mouth as I said it, "Mom, Dad, I know you guys are worried about leaving me to go on my own, trust me, I am as well, but this, *this* is our only chance. *My* only chance at getting closer to the truth. I've had this in my mind since I was *nine*, I even came crying to you guys about it. *Please.* Trust me, I'll have Kanzon and Daqpo with me. I know I'm a little bit careless, but they won't let anything happen to me. I give you, my word. If I stay here, the weirdos, whoever they are, will just come over to our house and destroy everything I know and love. I don't know how to explain it, but I *feel* it."

Usually, after one's kid would say something like this, his mom would probably say something like, "Oh, my little darling angel! Go! Go, make me proud, understand yourself. I trust you. Your dad and I trust you."

But my mom's quite different. Guess what she said?

"No. N plus O spells 'no'"

"What the biology, mom"

"How *dare* you say that to me? I am your *mother*."

My dad had to calm my mom down after that. I guess biology does have that effect on people.

I stared at my mom as if she'd just told me that Math wasn't real. Like, what else could I *possibly* say to convince her? There's a literal *stick* fused *inside* of me.

I was running out of options. I then turned my attention to my dad and looked at him with the eyes of a baby and then said, "Dad. Please."

He made a clueless face, and then we started communicating with our eyes while he was calming my mom down.

I'll give you a small gist of that eye conversation: Scary mom. Can't convince. Please. Ok.

My dad did that awkward cough thing and then started talking, "Babe, remember when we were kids—"

My mom shook my dad's calming hands off her and shouted, "Seriously? You too?"

"Just hear me out. Even I don't want him to go out alone like that, but I don't know, I kind of trust him with what he's saying."

"But what if he dies? Look at him!" she said, pointing at me.

"That *is* there, but if he says it's worth the risk, let it be. It'll all work out. Heck, his friend Gakpo—"

"Daqpo," I interrupted.
"—Daqpo's parents allowed him. We should as well."

"Please," he said.

"Please, mom," I added.

"You shut up," my mom shouted at me and then changed her attention to my dad, "Ugh...fine."

"LOVE YOU!" I went over to hug them both.

I think I could hear my parents snort and cry, but I preferred to ignore it because I can't handle emotions.

I said my byes and packed my bag to go over to Kanzon's for Step 3, but before I opened the door, my dad yelled from inside, "Hey, Yelix! Before you leave northward, come back here. I want to have a conversation with your little friends. You'll anyway cross us on the way."

"Ugh, okay! Love you both, bye!" I yelled back.

I smacked the door and travelled south towards Kanzon's, where I was hoping to see him already convinced by Daqpo.

I need to stop hoping for things which are too good to be true.

When I reached Kanzon's, I saw the most intense negotiation taking place.

Kanzon and Daqpo were sitting on opposite ends of a black metal table, with bases made of Kanzon's self-made pentagon-shaped wheels. Yeah, he was *that* smart. Bro was inventing stuff back when he was sixteen.

They were sitting on two praco-shaped chairs that Kanzon made just to make it so that I didn't sit on them, which really jarred me, but I chose to ignore it at that moment.

Both had their elbows on their table, with their heads resting on their crossed hands. It was akin to a business meeting.

Around their table were all of Kanzon's inventions, ranging from plasma thrusters to this thing called 'quantum weaponry', which I didn't understand, he donated to the Sosush Empire. I still don't know how all of that worked, but I was hoping to understand it over the course of this journey.

Kanzon was a person who moved into town back when I was in second grade, about nine years before all this happened. He was a silent guy who never really got along with people. He just wanted to be alone with his lab apparatus and instruments to make stuff, but sooner or later, Daqpo and I broke the barrier he'd made and became close friends with him.

If Daqpo was like a brother, Kanzon was like a close cousin, a cousin who only you could understand and have fun with. Even though we'd broken the barrier, he'd never told us about what happened with his parents; he always avoided that conversation.

All we knew was that they were alive till he was six years old, back when he resided in another galactic system. 'Something' happened there, which led to their death and him being sent to an orphanage in my galactic system. It was all a bit here and there, but we never really pestered him to tell us more because he always used to get visibly upset whenever the topic was brought up.

Kanzon was quite a handsome man, and I was pretty jealous of him for that. He had blonde and curly hair, blue eyes, a perfectly symmetrical face, and a rock-solid body. Like, how can you be smart *and* crazy good looking at the same time?

But yes, where was I? I entered the house using the unlocked door because knocking and ringing the bell seven times didn't work. I saw them sitting at that table, fully serious, and they didn't even notice me come in. Very unsafe security system for the house of a very smart dude.

"Why would you two buffoons want me with you for this adventure?" asked Kanzon.

"Because Yelix's the body, I'm the heart, and we *need* you,

Kanz, as the brain," said Daqpo.

"Since when were we body parts?"

Daq sighed. Did I mention that, for a very smart guy, Kanzon has a lot of trouble understanding metaphors, similes, and sarcasm?

"It's just a metaphor, man," Daq huffed, trying not to lose his temper, "We need someone as smart as you to complete the crew. Without you, we won't be able to travel, we won't be able to fight, we won't be able to do anything."

"And why's that?"

I could sense Daqpo losing his temper, so I had to intervene.

"Hi, guys!"

They both turned their heads simultaneously to look at me.

"Let's tone it down a bit, shall we?"

No response. There was this look in their eyes, a look of fear.

"What's wrong? You were just talking!"

Then I noticed something more. They weren't looking *at me*. They were looking *above* me.

And then I noticed it. A huge shadow. A shadow of something which would be approximately two feet above me was lurking over me, and to top it all off, upon focusing further, I noticed a certain hum.

My brain finally brained; I knew what the shadow was from.

"Oh biology," I muttered.

And then it grabbed me.

# CHAPTER IV

# Oh, for the love of Math...

'Why is all this happening to me?' became the only coherent thing in my mind as the predator put his gobby hands on me. I didn't know which one it was, but I wanted to put my bet on predator number three.

I was right!

The guy turned me around and said, "Harjan za Zecond likey...ma a pow..."

Ideally, I would've laughed.

But this time, it was different. I was so close to his face I thought he'd headbutt me if I laughed. Plus, he smelt absurd. I thanked Math that he was wearing a mask, else I probably would've suffocated.

"Ti ta di," he muttered ominously.

I couldn't understand a thing, but behind me, Kanzon shouted, "Yelix! It's a Vazhuru! They're people who thrive in the Gutter Plains! I'd give you a history lesson on them if we weren't on the verge of death. They're fast, strong, and big! *Very, very,* bad news."

"I KNOW THAT!" I yelled at him as my legs started feeling weightless.

"*These* were the guys I was telling you about," snarked Daqpo to Kanzon.

Kanzon shrugged.

"Guys, some help here?" I cried because I was seriously helpless.

I tried closing my eyes and clenching my fists like I did at the Fields of Srizure, but it just somehow didn't work this time. I was completely helpless, praying to Math as the Vazhuru predator tightened his grip on my love handles, and flung his head back, as if he was preparing to headbutt me.

Math delivered.

Before he could fling his head backwards to hit my face, I heard a little *PEUSH* behind me and saw a little beam of light go past my ear giving me a tingling sensation, straight into Harajan za Zecond's right cheek with a crackling hiss.

It was Kanzon's Plasma Rifle.

His grip loosened, and I set myself free, back rolling into the grasp of my two friends. I wasn't doomed after all.

"Eat my plasma dust, Gutter boy," yelled Kanzon.

Being rude was not his cup of ceasea – ceasea is like a daily beverage that we drink in Keo III.

I then set my eyes on Harjan za Zecond – actually, you know what? Now onwards I'll refer to him as HzZ. HzZ was somehow in perfect condition, sitting on the floor as if nothing had happened...and he looked angrier than ever – or at least, that's what I could make out from the way his eyes twitched.

"Give it a break, you humongous freak!" I bellowed at him. I don't know how I got myself to say that, because to be honest, my throat felt dry.

He growled back, and it sounded like a huge bell ringing.

I looked over to Kanzon, "Any tips, smarty pants?"

Kanzon shrugged, "There's not much that we know about Vazhurus except OH MY MATH."

"What's wrong?"

"LOOK," he pointed at HzZ.

As he'd asked me to do, I looked at HzZ. He was now wielding his sword – the same one I'd broken.

"No way," Daqpo, Kanzon, and I said simultaneously.

"Wait, why are you both saying "no way"?" Kanzon inquired.

"That's the sword I told you about, man," Daqpo groaned, "The one Yelix broke with whatever phenomenon happened in his body."

"Also wait, why are *you* saying "no way"?" I added.

"Because...because—" before Kanzon could finish, HzZ lunged. Can this guy *please* stop?

Just like before, he was coming with his sword over his head, ready to strike me down like a butcher striking praco meat (sidenote – while pracos are disgusting and scary, praco meat is *delicious*).
I tried doing the same thing *again*: closed my eyes and clenched my fists...no luck. I didn't feel the same surge of energy inside of me. I was so confused. Like, I could still feel the stick inside of me, but it just didn't work like it did before.

HzZ landed. We all jumped backwards to avoid the strike, which we somehow succeeded in doing. We saw as his shiny sword scraped through the wooden flooring and holy biology, he was *glowing*, glowing even more than he did at the Fields. He was *angry*.

He then placed it in a way that it was facing right in front of my face.

"Bro, there are two other people beside me. Try to hurt them as well, man, what's your obsession with me?" I tried to reason with him.

He just grunted back.

I couldn't see them, but I *knew* that Daq and Kan were giving me side-eyes for what I said. In the meantime, HzZ prepared to strike again. Daqpo stayed where he was, but Kanzon ran.

"Some help here, Kan?" Daqpo yelled at Kanzon.

No reply.

HzZ struck again. This time, I saved myself by ducking. I'm pretty sure his sword cut part of my hair, but at that point, I was just happy to be alive.

Daqpo threw some splintered to me, "Yelix, try sweating on this. Maybe this one will also start shining and...yeah, you know the rest."

Something inside me told me that this wouldn't work, but I still tried. I tried my best to get one drop of sweat off my body onto the stick for a good minute, whilst dodging HzZ's sword strikes at the same time. Here's a short summary of what was happening: he swung, I ducked. He growled, I sweated. Simple.

Finally, one fell.

HzZ stepped back for a moment, clearly terrified. That gave me some hope, maybe I wasn't doomed after all.

But no luck, even after the sweat fell on the splintered wood, the thing just didn't happen.

Daqpo and HzZ laughed, while Kanzon was nowhere to be seen.

"It was your idea, smelly," I hissed.

Daqpo put his hands over his mouth while HzZ continued.

Then, he started walking towards me.

"Oh Math," I muttered to myself.

He continued walking, and then it started – his sword started shapeshifting again, this time, into a trident.

"Bro, first you had a sword—" I jumped his first strike.

"—then a hammer—" I ducked his second strike.

"—then I broke that hammer—" I front rolled the third. He was starting to shine brighter than before.

"—then you had a sword again—" I barely dodged the fourth.

"—and now you have a trident—" I barely jumped over his strike.

"—what's next? A fork?—" He hit me this time. Not with his trident, but with his fists. He used a boxing combo of sorts, first he thrust the trident with one hand, which I dodged, then punched me with a right upper hook.

I fell to the ground.

He started laughing, "No pow bo di!"

He lined his trident up with my heart, ready to strike.

"De oa al."

I closed my eyes as he got ready to strike, expecting to die.

"No!" cried Daqpo.

I was ready to get stabbed.

Instead, all I felt were weird ashes on my body, so I opened my eyes.

I was staring *right* at HzZ with *nothing* in his hands.

"What...?" I mumbled.

And then I heard that PEUSH sound again and saw a bright line of light pass over me, straight into HzZ's forehead. I expected him to fall on me, so I wiggled out of the way, back to safety, to Daqpo.

He was still standing, but he looked...static, as if in shock at what had just happened.

Then I saw another one of those lines go over my head – it hit HzZ in the same spot as before, making his patterns glow less.

And another. This was the final hit. He fell.

Good thing I moved. Spontaneously, Daq and I turned back to see who it was, to check if it wasn't yet another adversary who came there to hunt us down for Math knows why.

Lucky for us, it was Kanzon holding his Plasma Rifle looking *cold*. I can't use a word except cold to describe the way he was looking so mysterious yet dumb yet smart yet intimidating yet...yeah, you get the point.

"Eat. My. Plasma. Dust," he said.

He had just saved my life, so I didn't make a snarky comment about how dumb he sounded when he said that.

We rushed to hug him.

"What happened?" inquired Daqpo.

"I need you guys to promise me that you won't tell this to *anyone*," Kanzon choked out. He was clearly struggling to say whatever he wanted to say, so Daq and I nodded.

"The...the Vazhuru..." his voice wavered. For the first time ever, Kanzon was afraid. It was something completely new to me. I wanted to press him, but before I could, he fainted.

# CHAPTER V

# Time to gear up!

Luckily, he didn't die, his pulse was still there. He was probably just really tired. Both of us breathed a breath of fresh air when we realized that.

Daq and I gave each other nervous looks.

I broke the silence, "What just happened?"

"I...I don't know, man."

"Surely, *surely* we didn't just commit murder...did we?"

"We...we did...but it was just self-defense. The Vazhuru attacked first."

"Well, I guess that's true but what in the biology do we do now?"

"I think..." he paused for a moment, looked at Kan's equipment, "...we grab some of *that*, pick our dear genius friend up, and take him straight to your home. The hospital is way too dangerous."

We did exactly that. We took one of his many gear bags and packed some gear. To be honest, we just picked stuff up at random because we did *not* know what the stuff did. Kanzon was a really organized man, so he had labels on quite literally *everything*.

This was our list of items:

1. two 'quantum shields' – pretty sure they were shields...just quantum, whatever that is,
2. three 'plasma rifles' – I think that was the cool stuff he killed HzZ with,
3. four 'nanite repair kits' – they had 'repair' in their name, that was enough for us to pick them up,
4. seven 'cryo-fog canisters' – they were small white cylinders which were freezing cold when I touched them,
5. six 'chrono bubbles' – they were small rainbow-coloured stickers, they seemed worthless, but I thought about the 'small size, big package' saying (probably fumbled that) and grabbed them, and lastly,
6. two 'dimensional bandoliers' – they were two grey spherical objects, but they sounded cool, so we grabbed them.

Along with all that, I grabbed a couple of his tools that were lying around so that he could build stuff along the way if he wanted to. It was his favorite pastime, so we thought why not?

Then, we skedaddled.

Or at least tried to skedaddle. Once we'd stuffed piñata of doom – the tool bag, the more important question came to mind: how in the world do we carry a medium-sized blonde?

It took us fifteen minutes to decide on the method we'd use to drag him home, but we finally decided on dragging him. It's time Kanzon got his legs dirty as well.

The entire journey was *quiet*. Neither of us uttered a word. We'd just killed a man and our friend was unconscious. For the first time, my yappathon brain was undermined by this feeling I couldn't name.

It took us longer than before because we were dragging a man and carrying a heavy tool bag *along* with our own bags, but once we reached home, it took us some time to ring the bell...not because our hands were full, but because we couldn't decide whether it was the right thing to do.

What if my parents call the medical center? What if they take away my permission to go northward? There were too many what ifs. Commendable indecisiveness by the two of us.

Then, I just said, "Man, let's just pray to Math and go ahead. Waiting won't help, we've anyway got Kan lying on the ground here."

I rang the bell.

Once we opened the door, my mom and dad had the most mom-dad reaction ever.

My mom yelled, "*Look* at the state of your shirt, young man. It hasn't even been *two hours* since we let you free."

Then my dad, calmly, sighed, "Heehat, maybe put your eyes on the kid that Daqpo and Yelix dragged back home?"

My mom shrieked when she realized Kanzon's unconscious body, "Is he dead?"

The look on her face was amazing, she had a mixture of 'scar*ed*-to-death mom' and 'scar*ing*-to-death mom' on her face. I would've laughed if the situation wasn't so serious.

Daqpo spluttered, "Uh, no ma'am! He was just a bit tired so he fainted."

My mom, clearly relieved now, exhaled, "Anlork, please pick him up and take him into the house...and you two," she turned her attention to us, "Get in."

Thank Math for my dad not caring much about my clothes, I guess, else Kanzon might've been lying on the ground for forty minutes.

Also, they were now in their normal home clothes: matching blue overalls...so I think my assumption of ruining their date *was* right.

Anyway, Daq and I swiftly went in with both our bags and Kanzon's extra heavy bag as well, because apparently, my dad can only carry so much on his shoulders.

Once we were in the house, I went straight over to the sofa and crashed on it. I didn't sleep, not because I didn't want to – Math, I wanted to – but because I couldn't till Kan woke up.

Daqpo was pretty much a daily visitor at my house, so he made himself comfortable quite quick. My mom was in the sofa room already and my dad joined us shortly after keeping Kanzon in my room to rest.

There was absolute silence – just the sound of wind from the outside and all the mechanical stuff working.

But obviously, my dad, who couldn't handle silence, broke it, "So, uh Daqpo, want anything to eat?"

Daqpo started fidgeting, and his eyes started darting to the kitchen, almost like a predator, "Uh, you know what, sir? I'll go and get some food myself. Thanks!" and he flew off and disappeared before I even knew it.

We shared a hatred for awkward conversations but, unfortunately, I knew I couldn't escape this one.

For a while, I got caught in my thoughts again. It wasn't usual for me to 'think', perse, but somehow, I was *actually* thinking about all the stuff that had happened on that day, and Seren's words were the first to come to my mind: The First. Were the Vazhurus after me? After 'The First'? Both? I really didn't know. I really, *really* needed to go meet this 'unraveller of entropy' as soon as possible.

I was about to go into another one of my 'zone-out' moments, but my mom started speaking.

"So, Mister Yelix, would you like to say anything?" she scoffed.

Silence. I couldn't open my mouth.

"Don't ignore your mom like that," commanded my dad.

I groaned, "Well, as you already knew, we went over to Kanzon's—"

"And almost got him killed, well done!" my mom grumbled.

"Mom, *please* let me finish," I snapped.

Bad decision.

"You will *not* shout at your mother like that, Yelix, apologize. Now," my dad shouted.

Well done, Dad, definitely winning the universal simping competition with that one.

"Sorry. My dear mother, could you please let me finish?" I said, my voice dripping with smugness.

"Go ahead, my lovely offspring," my mom responded. She knew how to fight back. No wonder my dad's so afraid of her.

I was just about to start when we heard a knock on the door.

I started shivering. What if it was one of the two Vazhurus? What if it was some other party interested in the same thing as the Vazhurus, whatever it was? What if...

My mom helped me escape my rabbit hole of 'what ifs' by talking once again, "I'll go get that."

"NO!" I yelled.

My mom looked at me confused, "What?"

"Let me go get it. Please."

"Okay?"

I went, my palms sweaty, knees weak, and arms heavy. I was taking little steps, to avoid whatever travesty was waiting behind the door. As I walked, the 'what ifs' kept flooding in: what if there's some mutated praco behind the door? What if there's some bounty hunter willing to kill to get me or 'The First'? I walked slow enough to the point where my dad had to yell, "Hey, kid! Pretty sure they'll leave before you get there."

Then, I obviously walked quicker and reached the door.

'Three. Two. One,' I counted in my head.

I opened it.

CHAPTER VI

# Yoohoo!

It was the Ceasea Man. He was standing there with a grin big enough to tear the universe in two, with his travel pod parked behind haphazardly, as always, humming with the blue energy that powered it.

I should've known better. It was six in the evening, that's *literally* when he comes every day. No wonder my parents weren't as terrified as me.

Uplatka the Ceasea Man was wearing his classic blue-green attire: a blue buttoned up and checkered shirt coupled with a green suspender, plain green trousers, and bright blue shoes. Along with that grin on his face, he rocked a perfectly groomed beard and glasses which covered his sea-green eyes.

Behind him, the street was quiet as always. All the symmetrical, brown, two story houses – just like ours – had the lights on but there was barely *any* sound. Everyone was either elsewhere, had left town, or was quietly chilling in their house.

"Yoohoo! Ah, Yelix! What a surprise! Rare to see you open the door!" he exclaimed.

You know what? This positive attitude on a very negative day was helping. So, I didn't mind it. It actually got a smile on my face.

"Here's your daily Uplatka's Ceasea delivery! A set of three," he continued.

My smile couldn't help but turn into a laugh because of his positive attitude, "Good to see you, Mister Uplatka! Thanks so much!"

I took the ceasea and started turning back but then another thought came to my head.

"Hmm, perchance, is it possible for us to have two extra today? We've got a few guests here and your ceasea is *the best* that I've *ever* had!" I gushed.

"Oh, why the biology not?"

He handed me two more of his special ceasea, rang the bell on his travel pod as always, and hollered, "Bye!"

Then, he went over to the next house. Math, I loved that guy's positivity.

I carried the ceasea box back in.

And then, in front of me, I saw a now perfectly fine Kanzon.

I dropped the ceasea box.

His clothes were dirty from Daq and me dragging him, and his eyes were scattered, as if he was scared about something or someone coming. His breathing was still...weird, like it was uneven, like he had an anxiety attack or something.

My dad understood what was happening. He rushed over to Kanzon, "Hey big guy, it's all good. You're at Yelix's house, don't worry. Everything's fine."

"Clean that up, mister," my mom yelled at me, and then shifted her attention to Kanzon, "Have a seat, Kanzon, you look really tired."

So, I cleaned the stuff up.

While cleaning, my mind circled around the same questions: why did Kanzon faint? Did he know something we didn't? What scared him? I was just...confused. Usually, one would be confused about him recovering so quickly, but that was the last thing on my mind. The day had been so weird already to the point where I was expecting the unexpected.

To get the answers to my question, I cleaned the pond of ceasea I'd created on the floor in a rush and sat on the sofa.

"DAQQQQQQQ!" I yelled, to get him in the sofa area from the kitchen as well. Mister Smelly Foody came from the kitchen with his hands full of packaged food.

There was absolute silence for a moment, again, but there was too much on my mind so I had to start.

"Kan, what were you trying to say to us before you...you know, fainted?" I asked him.

My mom scolded me for asking, "Yelix! He just woke up! Why are you pestering him?"

"It's okay, ma'am," Kanzon reassured, "It's just...Yelix, your parents don't have anything to do with the Sosush, right?"

"We hate them...no offence, Daq," assured my dad.

Daq gave an awkward smile to my dad. He really didn't like this situation.

Kanzon turned his attention to Daqpo, "Okay...well, Daq, please, for me, don't tell this to your parents...they're Senators of the Empire."

Daq hesitated, but he ended up saying, "Uh, okay, I guess?"

Kanzon looked at me, "Yelix, do your parents...know?"

I nodded. I was pretty sure that he was asking me about my parents knowing about the stuff that happened.

Kanzon continued, "Okay then. As I was saying, I highly request you all to ensure that this information doesn't go outside this room."

We all nodded. I really don't know why my parents were so interested, but they were there now so oh well.

Kanzon's voice was barely coming out of his throat, but he tried speaking, "The...the weapon that, that the Vazhuru was using...it was—"

He started coughing.

My mom gave me a look. A look that meant, 'Go get him a container of water, dumbo.'

And I did exactly that: rushed to the kitchen, filled a cup a water, ran back, dropped some of it on the way hoping that my mom would ignore it, and then gave it to Kan.

Kanzon started again, "Oh, much better. Thank you, guys. So, as I was saying, the weapon that the Vazhuru – Harjan za Zecond – was using, was some of the Quantum Weaponry I gave to—"

"The Sosush Empire," I interrupted.

He calmly continued, "Exactly...so the Sosush Empire is what is *actually* after that...thing in your bag, or you, or both..."

"Isn't it possible for the weaponry to have been, I don't know, robbed, or something?" Dad asked, out of curiosity.

"Mhm," Mom added.

"No, sir, ma'am, there were codes given to each weapon, which were only supposed to be shared with whoever wields them. The only people who had the codes were—" he looked at Daqpo.

"My parents," Daq muttered.

"Yeah, either they betrayed the Empire – which I highly doubt, because, from what I've seen, they're loyal servants of the emperor – or it was a direct order from the emperor."

"Holy biology," Daq and I mumbled in *absolute* sync.

Kanzon looked at Daq and me and continued, "Before I knew this, I wasn't planning to say yes to going with you guys...but this betrayal, this, this backstabbing...yes, I'll go. I made that weaponry to be used for good, not to have my two best friends...my only friends killed."

Damn. Who knew a smart guy could be good at emotions as well? Daq and I gave each other a look and then ran and hugged Kanzon. No one deserves to be betrayed like that.

"Thank you, guys," he mumbled under our tight grasps.

We kept hugging him till he yelled, "Hey, hey, hey! Let me go now, I don't want to faint again!"

We let out a laugh and let him go.

As I was going back to my seat, I saw mom and dad sitting on their sofas, smiling.

"So, Mom, Dad, are you fine with us going on this journey? I really want, *need*, answers about what happened three weeks ago, about what happened today, about...about *everything* since I was nine years old. I promise I won't get hurt,"

"And, and Kan and I are there with him!" Daqpo exclaimed.

Kanzon nodded.

My dad nodded and decided, "Alright, fine. We won't revoke the permission we gave you earlier today—" he looked at my mom, "—if that's fine with your mother."

My mom made a confused face but ended up saying, "Ugh, okay. But please, please take care," she looked at Daq and Kan, "Don't let *anything* happen to him, or to yourselves."

They nodded.

"Hmm, I think it's quite late now and you guys *visibly* look tired," my dad remarked, "It's better to rest up before doing something dangerous."

Mom added, "I agree with Anlork, have some food, sleep, then leave first thing tomorrow," she looked at the three of us, "Daqpo, Kanzon, sleep in Yelix's room. Yelix, sleep on the sofa today."

We nodded and did exactly what she did.

We dove into my mom's delicious food – some delicious praco meat – like hungry freaks who hadn't been fed for the past ten years, then crashed as soon as we hit our respective sleeping spots.

And then, she returned. Seren.

CHAPTER VII

# What in the biology is happening in this universe?

Ah! Of course! Make an already confusing day even more confusing!

As soon as I closed my eyes, I went back into the void and saw *her*. Seren. She was there, beautiful and other-worldly as always, staring at me.

The void was also the same as always – an area of absolute nothingness, there's not much else to add to it. It was nothing and everything at the same time.

Seren started speaking, her voice as soothing as the last time, "So, you know."

I stayed quiet. Not because I wanted to, but because I thought I couldn't speak.

"You can speak," she stated.

I tried opening my mouth, expecting it to stay shut like it did the last time I was here, but, to my surprise, it worked.

"What do you mean, 'you know'?" I asked her.

"About yourself, Arbiter of Gravity."

"What of what?"

"So, you don't."

I was losing my temper; I mean, it was tough to lose it in front of such a woman but holy biology I'd had enough, "Stop being so mysterious, woman."

She looked visibly hurt, and she didn't say a thing.

"Uh, sorry, please, Seren, tell me what I don't know," I said, calmly this time.

"No, no, I can't," she started frantically walking in the void, "It isn't my place to tell you...how, how do you not know?"

"Calm down," I tried walking towards her, my legs somehow working this time, "How can I get to know whatever it is that I must know?"

She shrieked, making a sound that made my heart skip a beat and started holding her head, as if in pain.

I went over to her and yelled, "Seren! What's wrong?"

"Yelix...I...I...argh!" she made the same sound again.

"What's happening?"

I was starting to get worried. I didn't even know her that well but there was...there was some kind of connection I felt with her, which somehow made me care.

"Yelix...just...ack!" another worrying sound.

She started flickering, like a dying star. My heart was pounding more than the ground when HzZ stepped on it earlier today.

I put my hands on her shoulder, "Whatever it is, Seren, it'll be okay, don't worry."

I couldn't believe the words coming out of my mouth, to be honest. I never really was a serious guy, so this was pretty new to me.

As soon as our skins touched, I felt this weird warmth...a warmth that made me feel like everything would be okay. That warmth was gentle yet overwhelming, it felt like the crimson-red haze of Keo III had moved away and we finally felt the stars' light. I'm sure that she felt it too because I could *feel* her calming down.

She stopped flickering, and she let her hands off her head.

"What...happened?" I asked.

"The Dominion...they have them. They have The Second and Third. You need to hurry. Reach the Unraveller. *Quick.*"

She sounded serious, yet also scared, and I should've closed my eyes, but I just couldn't until...until I knew.

"Are you okay now?" I asked.

She smiled, "Yes, thank you."

Her eyes shone brighter than a star.

"Uh, okay, I guess."

"You seem confused..."

"What is this 'First', 'Second', and 'Third' that you talk about?"

"You'll know when you reach the unraveller. Now go, close your eyes, and you shall wake up," she commanded.

I couldn't help but do what she asked.

Still confused, I closed my eyes.

The next thing I knew, I was awake. My body felt fresh, all the lethargy from the previous day was weirdly...*gone*. It just wasn't there. I was ready to walk a thousand miles, dodge a million more quantum weapon strikes, get attacked by a billion more Vazhurus, and...no, I wasn't ready to get chased by a trillion pracos. They're very scary.

But every positive comes with a balancing negative. Now, to add to the multiple questions that were already in my head, Missus Perfect, Seren, added more: what the biology is 'the Dominion' and for the love of Math what is it that I must know that *she* can't tell me? Like, help me out, here.

*Anyway*, it was six in the morning, and I realized that I'd woken up six hours before my usual wakeup time – yeah, I'm lazy, so what? It's the holiday season.

I got up – still on the sofa, just not laying down anymore. When I got up, the first thing I saw was my parents, sitting on the sofas.

They were in the same clothes as yesterday, which was expected, and were whispering to each other.

My dad looked...anxious, like, he had that tell, you know? His leg was shaking on the ground, up-down-up-down-repeat, while my mom looked like she'd aged ten years – not because her makeup was off, but because she had those worry-wrinkle lines on her face.

To state the obvious, they were worried; their whispers were faint, but the weight of the worry was *heavy*, to the point where they didn't even notice the fact that I was awake.

"Good morning, Mom, Dad," I said, lightly.

They looked at me like I was an alien.

"How are you awake so early?" asked my mom, clearly surprised looking at their boy, who had a messed-up sleep schedule, waking up on time.

"I don't know, just..." I drifted away, thinking of all those questions again, thinking of whether I'll be able to manage myself or not, thinking of...yeah, you get the point.

"Just nervous," I confessed.

They knew it wasn't like me to feel negative emotions, it was a rare feeling for me, and an even rarer sight for them.

"It'll be all okay, Yelix, you just need to believe in yourself—" my dad assured me.

"And yes, you might have this new type of...power, or something, whatever it is you told us about, but you need courage to continue," said my mum, who was positive for the first time in a while.

"Strength is earned, but courage is chosen," added my dad.

"How did you come up with that then," my mum joked.

"I don't know."

I couldn't help but smile.

"That's our boy!" exclaimed my mom and dad in sync.

Their reassurance, their shocking positivity, and their playful banter added *some* positivity to my then-negative mind.

I went to hug them. Something inside me told me that this would be the last time for a good while. Their warmth was everything to me, it was even more calming than whatever I felt with Seren.

Family. There's nothing like it.

Of course, to ruin the good moment, reality came back to hit me like the pracos in my dreams.

Behind me, I heard Kanzon, "Good morning, sir, ma'am, and Yelix, it's time we move."

I couldn't help but yell, "*Already*?"

Daqpo, Mister Smelly Foody, also yelled from inside the room, "WHAT ABOUT BREAKFAST?"

The nerd replied with the nerdiest reply possible on Nerdyland, "I prepared the required food yesterday after everyone dozed off and packed it into my dimensional bandoliers. We have no time, we must move. The Sosush are persistent; before we know it, they'll attack the house, and we do not want that."

"Uh, okay," I gulped, "What about travel? We have to go back to your place, right?"

"Not required. You guys were extremely lucky, one of the dimensional bandoliers you packed already *had* one of my travel pods. We must move whilst luck is on our side."

"Won't you need a map?" my mom asked.

"All up here!" I exclaimed whilst pointing at my head.

"Well, I guess you should do what the smartest of you lot said." my dad said, a hint of disappointment in his voice.

I looked at my parents, I knew that watching me go would have a big toll on them, "Mom, Dad, I promise I'll be back soon. It'll all be okay."

They nodded. We shared another hug, they both kissed me on my forehead, shook the other guys' hands, and then we skedaddled.

It's time for an adventure. Whatever was ahead of us – the Unraveller, the Sosush, the Dominion – they didn't know what was coming...I mean, they probably did, but I'll just say that for dramatic effect.

# CHAPTER VIII

# And so, it begins.

Genuinely speaking, I was expecting an ambush when I stepped out the door, to the point where I took at least five on-the-spot circles to check for any lurkers. There was no one, and Daqpo was laughing at me while Kanzon was looking at me with an embarrassed face, so I stopped.

As soon as I stopped, Kanzon spoke, "So, guys, should we begin?"

Daq and I nodded.

Immediately after, Kanzon started fiddling with the gear bag we brought him, mumbling some technical terms that I didn't understand, like, what is a pocket dimension?

As he did that, I looked around the neighborhood...which was quite boring because it was the same as always – crimson red haze, dark black clouds, and barely any light other than the stuff coming out of the houses. Lifeless. So, I decided to watch as Mister Smelly Foody gobbled through an entire packet of packaged greens. I didn't understand his stomach, because how in the Math can one person eat so much but still stay relatively fit? This was even more confusing than whatever happened the previous day. What made it worse was that he didn't even realize that I was looking at him eat...that's how bad his obsession was.

Daqpo was wearing this stupid shirt that said 'Who's the SMARTEST of them all' – clearly not him – in red, with a pure black base color. Along with that, he wore some black lowers with black shoes. Quite a basic fit, but the food was starting to ruin it. Did I mention he's a very shabby eater?

I sighed and turned my attention to Kanzon, who looked extremely goofy working with mechanical things wearing clothes that a person would probably wear while going to a nine to five, sort of like my dad – a brown shirt, black trousers, and brown formal shoes. It was time to bother him.

I asked him, "How much time is it going to take, Kan?"

He kept fiddling with his mechanical parts, ignoring me.

I was pretty sure he didn't hear me, so I yelled this time, "HOW MUCH TIME IS IT GOING TO TAKE, KAN?"

He turned around to look at me. His face was covered by the fire-repellent thing that mechanics use, but I could *feel* the annoyance radiating off him, "My *amazing* friend Yelix, ideally, it should've taken me less than one minute, however, since you and my other *great* friend, Daqpo, packed the gear bag like lunatics, it'll take me about...three more minutes to fix the mess you've made. Wait, *patiently.*"

"Alright, man, dang," I muttered.

So, we waited. There was nothing else that we could do, really. Daqpo, without a care in the world, kept munching down whatever he was having, while I kept looking around like a scout, *waiting* for someone to ambush us.

After what felt like forever (which was probably just two minutes), Kanzon straightened up, brushed off his hands like he was an action model and a smile formed on his face. He was beaming with happiness – a rare sight for me.

"Finally!" he yelled as if to inform the whole neighborhood.

I didn't understand what he was so happy about because I literally could not see a thing.

"Uh...where's the pod, Kan?" I asked politely, afraid of him giving me one of his lectures again.

He put his hands in the bag, took out one of the two spherical objects we'd packed...dimensional bandoliers, I think, then, put his hands inside that thing quite oddly, like, it was so small but somehow, he could fit his entire hand in there and yet not feel any pain, as if there was infinite space underneath.

He spent a good few seconds doing that, until he took out a little toy ship, yelling, "Ta-da!"

He held the toy ship up as if it was the crown jewel of the universe. Internally, I thought, 'I have many of those, what's so special about this?' but that's when I looked a bit closer. It was much more detailed than whatever I had.

I couldn't help but ask, "Is this it?"

Kanzon made a disgusted face as if I asked a very repugnant question.

"This is a compact pod," he started, and his disgusted face quickly turned into a smile, clearly proud of whatever he'd made, "It makes use of Quantum Superposition to collapse all structural components into a compact state when not in use. When activated, quantum tunnelling—"

He stopped, looking at our faces getting rapidly more clueless and confused.

"Okay, you know what, I'll simplify it for you guys: this little baby is the Arnazt 7. It makes use of some advanced physics principles to make it small when I'm not using it, big when I am. I would start explaining Zero-Point Energy – the energy that essentially gives it infinitesimal running capabilities – but that would be a bit too complex for you guys," he continued, smiling a bit less than before, but still visibly proud.

As soon as he finished, Daq and I, in complete sync, did the sarcastic slow clap.

He made the frustration sound, "Argh," and then muttered, "Just look at the magic...or should I say Science?"

"Alright then, Smarty Pants," I thought motivating him might help, "Show us what you've got!"

He pressed a button on the toy ship and then threw it on the street.

"Woah," I couldn't help but maintain my excitement, "Finally, something interesting in this dead neighborhood."

Mid-air, the ship rapidly grew, flickering whilst it happened, turning into a real-sized pod. As it grew, I could feel the environment grow hot, as if it was emitting some silent energy. The pod was elliptical in shape and oh my Math was it *majestic* – there wasn't any other word for it. It was shining with a cyan aura, with its core colored in a light shade of blue. The pod was full of random designs – some parabolas, some cubic graphs – stuff I noticed from my math classes. On top of all that, the ship was silent; it didn't make a single sound, different to every other pod I'd ever seen before. Whatever the 'Zero-Point Energy' was, it was fascinating. Somehow, it didn't even have that usual-pod smell: a smell that'll make your nose burn.

In the middle, in a deep red color, was the pod's name: '*Arnazt 7*', it was in a font more jarring than the one I used in my sixth-grade biology presentation (I hated the subject with a passion), but then my eyes went to the most important part: K. D. Y. He had that drawn on his pod. I couldn't believe that *we* meant so much to him, to the point where he put us down on his creation.

"Not bad," Daqpo snarked, "My snack hologram projector is better though."

I smacked the back of his head *hard* and made him turn his attention to the three initials.

He gulped, "Uh, great stuff, Kan!"

Then, we went over to Kanzon, who was standing there with his hands on his waist, and his chest pumping out, staring at his creation.

I raised my eyebrow, "Hmmm, so, Kan, K. D. Y., huh?"

Kanzon looked confused, "Huh?"

I pointed at it, "*K. D. Y.?* Ring any bells?"

"Oh! That? Yeah, I just did that to fill the space; don't think huge, shut up and get into the thing," he pointed at what looked like the entrance.

"Mhm, sure," Daqpo muttered as he started moving towards the entrance.

"As you say, milord," I grumbled as I followed Daq.

Kanzon collected his bags and then came right behind me.

The doors opened automatically as soon as we got in close proximity to them, and it was empty.

I went in expecting some absolute madness, like hovering sofas, a mixed drink bar, and at least a billion seats, but nope.

It was empty: five brown seats, one fancy control desk, and black walls and flooring, with some little windows.
"Uh, yeah, the outside's quite cool but the inside is...yeah, sorry guys," he said, rubbing his hand on the back

of his head out of embarrassment.

"Hey, man, at least we have something, don't say sorry," I told him, trying to sound supportive.

"Yeah, bro, don't say sorry," mumbled Daqpo, his mouth still full of food with one of his hands still in the packet, and the other now on Kanzon, to support him.

"Alright, then, I guess," said Kan, "Strap in."

He slid into the control seat, while Daq and I sat on the two seats around him. I was expecting some crazy tech-y thing to happen when I sat, but nothing did, they were just basic chairs. They were comfy, though, so I didn't really mind them. Daq *finally* got done with his food for the time being so he threw it in the bin below the control center.

"This is going to be a smooth ride, unless, of course, the Sosush send another one of their attacking squads behind us or some other party interested in you, the shiny thing, or both, does something similar," Kanzon declared.

That instantly reminded me of what Seren said: the Dominion...what in the world is it? And how do they have 'The Second' and 'The Third'? What could they have possibly done? Why was Seren so scar—*ZOOOOOOM*; before I could finish my thoughts, the pod started moving at crazy speeds. I hit my head on the soft chair cover, but the momentum was so high that the impact couldn't get cushioned.

"Could've warned us there," grumbled Daq.

I agreed, "Yeah, that hurt."

"Sorry, boys!" Kanzon laughed.

But then confusion struck me: how would Kanzon know where to even go? The map is in *my* head; not his, so I had to ask him, "Anyway, do you even know where we have to go, bro?"

"Nope, but you said northward so that's where I'll move. Keep a lookout for shadowy-looking establishments, maybe," he replied.

I closed my eyes to once again look at that star map that had entered my mind; I was still placed on one of the shinier stars even though I wasn't in the Fields anymore. Clearly, that shiny star signified me. I don't know why it took me so much time to understand that.

Anyway, I focused further and looked at the north side of that peculiar map as we continued moving. Right ahead of me, ahead of what seemed like Dezisk's Hills, I saw another bright star which was now...flickering. My heart skipped a beat, flickering is *not* good, is what I've learnt from my experiences so far, so I knew that we *had* to hurry.

"Kanzon, the Unraveller is right after Dezisk's Hills. How much time will we reach there in?" I asked hurriedly.

"Hey, hey, calm down, man. According to my calculations, we'll get there in about two hours, chill," Kan assured.

I took a deep breath for a second after Kan's reassuring words.

While Kanzon did some stuff I could barely understand with the controls, I thought I'd talk to Daqpo...but he was too busy eating again, so I decided to look out the windows, over to the constantly moving scenery. Of course, it was moving relative to me only since we were the ones moving but...yeah, you get the point. In the blurry environment, I could see beautiful greenery, colorful flowers, and so many different types of creatures I could barely see on a normal day.

I saw parasktis, viziks, ranvods, and ayzaks.

Parasktis bounced through the fauna with more energy than my dad after an energy drink, their four oversized ears moving up and down constantly. I noticed their small eyes, and it confused me like crazy because how in the biology were they able to see anything?

Behind them, viziks followed with their narrow faces scanning the temperature to decide whether their tail should be made of ice or fire.

Ranvods were sitting peacefully, looking like oversized pink humans – the sight was both calming and wholesome, yet eerie, like pracos minus all the terror.

Then, on top of the Hills, ayzaks stood motionless with their thick white fur perfectly contrasting the black clouds. They looked down on us like guardians of Dezisk's Hills.

The sight of ayzaks meant that one had officially entered Dezisk's Hills. Dezisk's Hills weren't anything special, they were just named after the first emperor of the Sosush Empire, Dezisk, and were one of the biggest tourist attractions of the planet.

Entrance in Dezisk's Hills meant that we were only about half an hour away and that, for the first time *ever*, I spent an hour and thirty without talking smack about Daqpo or not thinking about The First, the Dominion, or Seren.

I cheered, "Ayyy! We're so close!"

"I'd hold my celebrations if I were you, Yelix," warned Kanzon.

"What's wrong now?" moaned Daqpo.

As he said that, I heard a sound I'd last heard in my dreams...no, it couldn't be.

"There are some spatial anomalies – unusual stuff around us – being detected by the pod..." said Kanzon, his voice filled with fear.

It got louder, the sound...the terrifying, shiver-inducing screech...there was no way that they were here; they couldn't be.

Just as I thought that stuff, the pod halted to a stop all of a sudden.

Math bless Kanzon for a good protective infrastructure inside his pod, else I might've crashed *right* into the control center of the ship.

Around me, the sounds I was hearing got louder. I could see Daqpo and Kanzon's faces tense.

I knew exactly what the spatial anomalies were.

The sound was the cry of pracos.

"Why did you stop? The sound! It's...it's the pracos! The spatial anomalies are those disgusting scary ogres!" I yelled at Kanzon.

"It wasn't me! I promise I didn't stop the pod," he yelled back.

"Then who was it?" Daqpo yelled as well.

Kanzon looked over to the control center, and I saw fear creep up on his face. Then, without saying a word, he put his hands into the gear bag we'd packed for him and started passing some of the stuff to us – the rifle, the canisters, you name it.

"Can you tell us, Kan?" Daq barked at Kan.

Ignoring Daqpo, Kanzon gulped, "Ready to use your powers, Yelix?"

Before I could say a thing, I saw the front of the pod get torn apart.

Pracos – five of them, were there, disgusting as ever, and ready to destroy us.

# CHAPTER IX

# I'm not that useless...am I?

This was my worst nightmare. Pracos, edge of a hilly path, feeling powerless, you name it.

As soon as the five pracos ripped apart our pod and stared at us in the eyes, I was *done*. I knew I couldn't help the boys, I just...I felt powerless.

I felt powerless to the point where I couldn't even hold the stuff that Kanzon threw over to me. The shield? Dropped it. The rifle? Missed it. Three of those canister thingies? Grabbed them, then dropped them, freezing the ground. So *that's* why they were so freezing cold.

My heart was pounding. I'd never been so afraid before, like, the Vazhurus' ambush was *nothing* in comparison to whatever this was. The air rapidly started to become heavier, and I was starting to lose sense of myself.

But then, to make matters worse, they charged. However, unlike my dreams, they didn't charge like wild maniacs – they were walking, as if they wanted to play with us. This 'play with us' thing was starting to get a bit too common, like first the Vazhurus and now these things as well...? We weren't *that* weak – I mean, we were, but still. As they walked in, their disgusting smell spread across the pod, even the open front area couldn't save us from that smell. Not bringing my Fields mask was a wrong decision.

As soon as they started walking in, I lost my balance; I fell to the ground, butt first. Normally, Daqpo would've laughed, but the situation was way too tense for him as well.

That's when the first domino dropped.

Kanzon took the first shot with his Plasma Rifle. Ayzakseye (that's what we say when you hit the target, by the way). Straight through the head, making the first praco fall in an instant. How was this guy a genius, probably the most handsome guy I'd ever seen, humorous, *and* also a champion marksman? Is there anything he could not do?

Along with adding so many questions in my head, he did add one more thing: hope. I finally saw an outcome where we *don't* get turned into the pracos' dinner.

Kanzon shot another. Ayzakseye. Down.

Then, to my absolute surprise, Daqpo shot one as well. Obviously, not an ayzakseye, but he still downed one in five shots – two shots on two of its seven arms, two on two of its five eyes, and then one last shot on its disfigured nose. I couldn't help but be proud of him.

Seeing Daqpo actually being able to do something made me feel less powerless, if that made sense. I could finally feel my breath calming down, my arms not feeling like some minced praco meat, my legs finally feeling like...my legs. After what felt like a miracle, I got up.

*PEUSH. PEUSH. PEUSH.* I picked the rifle that I'd missed and shot one of the two last pracos on its crooked lips, one of its many arms, and then its small, disfigured nose. I felt one of the craziest surges of energy, not as crazy as that day on the Fields, obviously, but still *crazy*. I'd just murdered a living being for the first time ever. I felt guilty but at the same time, pracos didn't really count as living beings to me personally, they were just...eh, so I was fine with shooting them.

Another one. *PEUSH*. This time, I hit the ayzakseye.

I couldn't believe it.

"Guys...how did we just manage that?" I mumbled, still not being able to believe what we'd just done.

Kanzon exhaled, "I don't know *how* we did it, but what I do know is that we're now stran—"

He got interrupted by Daqpo's scream.

We had spoken a bit too soon. In the far distance, there were more – ten more pracos, on their way. The difference this time? They were charging. Charging with rocks and other throwables – just like in my dreams.

Their movements were random and quick – one moment, one praco was at the left-most spot, but then the next, it was somewhere in the middle.

Seeing them charge made me lose balance again, but I contained myself this time – if we could handle five of them, we could *easily* handle ten of them.

I was wrong. We started shooting at them like maniacs, but the shots just didn't hit.

While shooting, Kan yelled, "Guys! Don't worry about ammunition! It's infinite! Just ensure that you don't shoot continuously for too long, else it might overheat!"

Did I ever mention how Daq was *horrible* at following commands?

While Kan and I were shooting calmly, sort of like *PEUSH. PEUSH. PEUSH. PEUSH.*, Mister Smelly Foody was shooting like *PEUSHPEUSHPEUSHPEUSH.*

His rifle overheated in no time, making him throw it off the hill like an absolute dumbhead.

"Daq! Use a shield to...well, shield us! It's got Quantum Principles! It'll absorb the impact of the projectiles and absorb all the energy!" Kanzon shouted, his voice *barely* making it out of all the *PEUSH.*s, *THUCK.*s, and screeching sounds.

Daq, clearly clueless, "How does that even—"

"Don't ask questions! Just hold it up! The shield knows what to do better than you," Kan snapped, his voice full of frustration.

"Where's your shield, Yelix?" Daq asked me while scrambling on the floor of the pod.

I groaned, "Didn't Kan give you one—"

Daq interrupted me, "I threw it away with my rifle!"

"It's behind me! Get it *now*, fool!" I barked.

He tried crawling behind but then he bumped into me, making me fall to my knees mid-shot, shooting Kanzon's leg in the process, making him fall as well.

"Sorry!" I yelled as he and I both fell, back and chest first respectively.

We were now completely useless. The horde was on its way, coming towards us ever so quickly while the three of us were the most dysfunctional team *ever*.

Projectiles kept getting thrown at us, *THUCK. THUCK. THUCK.*, while Kanzon was groaning in pain.

Even in pain, Kanzon tried commanding us, "Daq! Get the shield and protect me! Take my gun and give cover fire! Yelix – go to my gearbag and get one of my nanite repaire kits – the ones with a little plus on them!"

We did exactly that. Even though I was shaken to my core, I couldn't let my friends get hurt. I hurried over to the bag and grabbed what Kan had asked me to grab, while Daq grabbed the shield and put it over Kan and himself.

I passed the little kit to Kan who just threw it over the place he got shot and then boom, some little automatic squares started moving and sealing his wound, weaving his skin and other boring biological stuff back together with a faint blue glow and strong hum. Within milliseconds, the bleeding stopped, and his leg looked as good as new, except the fact that his trousers were now torn and that there was a scar on his leg.

In front of him, I saw Daqpo desperately holding the shield up high to protect himself and Kan.

The shield had started glowing, probably because it was absorbing the energy, or whichever Physics thingie majingie was happening.

Kan yelled, "Daqpo, aim it at them and push the button at the back *now*!"

Daqpo did exactly that and *woah*.

The shield shined with a beam of light so strong that it almost blinded me. I was ninety-nine point nine nine per cent sure that the light would've destroyed those obscene pracos.

It didn't.

They kept coming at us; they perfectly jumped the massive beam of light.

Yeah, now we were definitely done for.

Kanzon looked at Daqpo and I and saw the look on our faces, "Guys, it's not over. I have something else in my gear bag which—Daqpo you absolute—argh!"

He put his head in his hands.

In front of us, right where I'd kept his gear bag, lay a set of ashes.

The shield's beam of light burnt the bag – all of the gear we'd packed from Kanzon's place was now *nothing*.

We were doomed.

I closed my eyes to try and unlock that stick-energy as a last-ditch effort as the pracos charged, but nope! I couldn't feel that surge of energy.

I kept trying but no luck. I could feel the projectiles hitting me, but I obviously couldn't see them.

We had no protection other than the last two plasma rifles and one shield, both of which yielded nothing – the rifle shots didn't hit, and the shield was on a cooldown.

I'd lost all hope. Daqpo and Kanzon were silent as well.

We waited. Silent. Helpless. Waiting for the end as the pracos' screeching noises got closer, their seven legs shaking the ground as they got near.

Just then, through my closed eyes, I felt that black screen you see when your eyes are closed turn lighter. I thought I died so I decided to slap myself.

Nope, still alive.

I opened my eyes and immediately shut them again. A blinding white light came down from above, even brighter than Seren. My heart raced – was it a new enemy? A miracle?

Then I noticed the ground under me vanish, replaced by a weightless pull. I wasn't sitting in the Arnazt 7 anymore, I was flying, floating. The pracos' sounds started turning distant, and I couldn't feel their projectiles landing on me anymore. The sound got replaced by this strange hum, an almost mechanical sound, which rapidly grew closer as time passed. I wanted to look up to see who or what was pulling me, but the light was too intense.

Were we getting saved? Or did another enemy await us on the other side of the glow?

I didn't care. Anything was better than being praco chow.

CHAPTER X

# The Ishazto.

As we got pulled further, I started seeing what was pulling us up: a massive ship, red in color with a design that I could recognize from my history and politics classes, along with the many times I'd been to Daqpo's place.

It was an emblem, of sorts, covering at least half of the bottom of the huge ship which was *at least* hundred times the size of a Vazhuru in length. The emblem was in a hexagonal shape with little orbs that were interlocked with each other, surrounded by curly lines. It stood out with its bluish-purple glow which perfectly contrasted its dark background and the ship's dark red base. The emblem was surrounded by spiky formations, probably to assert dominance. I remembered, from the textbooks, that this emblem wasn't just an insignia. It was a warning. A promise of destruction.

I knew exactly where we were going.

The Sosush Empire's mobile fortress, the Ishaztos. The Ishaztos wasn't just a ship – it was akin to a moving planet.

We kept going closer and I started seeing new details of the Ishaztos, details that made my stomach churn.

There were two massive rectangular shapes poking out of the bottom – guns, guns with the ability to destroy entire fleets, planets, and much more. Along with those two massive rectangular shapes were smaller rectangles, various of them. These were definitely the low energy blasters. No wonder the Sosush were the supreme power of two entire galactic systems. They were a force to be reckoned with.

The Ishaztos made me feel small, insignificant. It was a reminder of insignificant we were, a reminder of how we could be wiped out by possibly a single press of a button.

I knew what they wanted: me, or the rock, or possibly both. That made me feel this heart-wrecking surge of guilt, because all of this was happening because of *me*, or because of the rock in *my* possession. Why did I get my poor friends involved in this? Their lives, their happiness, *everything* was at stake because of *me*. I couldn't get myself to look at them, because looking at their terrified faces just made the guilt hit harder.

To get me out of my rabbit hole, I felt a change in environment. The light around us dimmed as we neared the underside of the ship – a loud hum made my body vibrate and my ears want to chop themselves off my body to escape. The moment we crossed the threshold, the weightless pull disappeared, and we crashed onto a hard, metallic floor making a loud *THM.* sound, butt first.

In front of me, was a massive, golden throne with the Sosush Empire's emblem etched on it. Around it was four more seats – seats for the senators and generals, that mean's two of them belonged to Daqpo's parents. As I looked around, I saw the sheer vastness of the room, there was so much area with absolutely nothing. The walls glowed with the same faint bluish-purple shine as the emblem and had some peculiar flickering designs, giving me chills. I then looked down – the floor was the same dark red metallic color as the external of the ship.

I turned my head backwards and saw a long empty hall with a similar design, going into a 'T' intersection.

There was not a single entity in the vicinity.

I turned my attention to Kanzon and Daqpo, "Guys, let's run!"

They both looked at me with confused faces.

"What?" I asked, confused about their confused faces.

"Yelix, how do you plan to escape one of the most powerful ships in the universe?" Kanzon inquired.

"You know, uh...you do something then Daqpo does something then I do something then boom! Escape plan," I replied.

"Right, so a whole bunch of nothing, then," Kanzon grumbled.

"Guys..." Daqpo started, his face looking guilty, "Let's just...wait."

"What's wrong?" I immediately asked. It was odd seeing him like that, he was always the jolly good guy so this scared me.

"Nothing," he looked down, "It's just...I think we're here because of me...If I hadn't made...if I hadn't made Yelix fall, maybe we wouldn't—"

I knew what he was talking about, I really wanted to assure him that it was a group mistake. *We* were dysfunctional, not just him alone. However, before he could end or I could start, he got interrupted by footsteps in the background.

Slow, heavy *thuck.* sounds in close unison.

The sounds echoed through the empty halls, and I could hear them inching closer as moments passed. I wanted to get up but then I recalled what Daqpo said: 'Let's just...wait.'

His parents were senators for the Sosush, so he knew some stuff that we didn't. He knew how dangerous they were, he knew which tactics worked, and which didn't – so I stayed down, as did the other boys. We waited for what sounded like the council to walk past us and sit on their seats.

First to walk by us was the male general. He was about as tall as my dad and was *wham.* He wielded a sword and shield. The sword was something I'd seen before – it was the sword that HzZ used. Ideally, I would've shared a look with Daqpo, but that time I thought I'd get impaled even if I moved. He sat on the chair nearest to me, the leftmost.

Behind him followed a chirpy young woman, who I couldn't believe was the female general. She hopped around like a giddy young girl and sat on the rightmost seat, nearest to Daqpo. The seat looked *way* too big for her short and thin build. She was wielding a flail, a flail which moved quite irregularly – like, the chain was sometimes very long, sometimes very short.

Both the generals were wearing the same outfit: dark red armor which emitted that *same* bluish-purple glow. The armor looked unbreakable, further spreading their dominant aura.

Now, how did I know that they were the generals?

Well, I knew because they weren't Daqpo's parents – the senators, who were the next to enter.

Both the senators entered at the same time, Daqpo's mom passed him, and his dad passed me. They both wore this big gown – dark red in color, with the same glow. They walked royally, completely opposite to Daqpo, i.e., they actually watched their steps and didn't change their directions randomly.

I saw as his dad sat on the seat behind the male general, while the mom sat on the seat parallel to him, emitting a crazy amount of aura.

As soon as they sat, they saw our faces and their jaws dropped. They probably couldn't believe that *we* were the people who got caught – their son and his friends.

The reaction lasted quite short, however, because the emperor came in.

Notice how I didn't say walked in? Yeah, that's because he flew in. Emperor Aanzshat was wearing a mixture of the generals' and the senators' uniform: a dark red armored gown. He looked, both, scary *and* royal.

He flew in in the sense that he wasn't exactly walking – below his feet were some thrusters which made him float in the air. To make matters even more crazy, he could control the power of the thrusters.

He hovered right over the three of us, making a mess of all our hair, came back to normal height – near the floor, basically, and then continued over to his throne at a speed slower than that of an ayzak.

Mister Aashtus's blue eyes were *wide* open, and I could see his huge nose go crazy because of the anxiety, while his lips were usually barely visible because of his huge white beard. He was rocking white hair, which perfectly contrasted his wife, Missus Shrizas' black hair. Her face was full of makeup and her multicolored – green and blue – eyes looked just as weird as her multicolored red and yellow hair.

In front of them, the male general was twirling his moustache, whilst his fiery red eyes stared me down as if I was some untouchable. I couldn't help but at least give a small smile looking at his bald head.

Then, there was the female general who was busy playing with her flail. Unlike the other women I'd seen in my life, minus Seren, she wasn't wearing any makeup or other products; her brown eyes and curly hair looked perfectly natural.

At last, the emperor reached his throne and sat, while Daq's parents' face went back to jaw-dropped mode.

As soon as he sat, I could feel the air in the room getting denser, as if the already tense situation had gotten ten times more tense.

If the male general was huge, Aanzshat was *massive*. Even while sitting, he looked bigger than my dad, but if his body was scary, his face was just *scarier*: it was unnaturally symmetrical, more than Kanzon, and it was full of scars. A purple eye patch covered one of his eyes and his lips were more crooked than the nose of a praco. On top of his head, a dark red crown with the same glow as his armor pressed down on his blonde, massive low taper fade.

"So, we finally meet," announced Emperor Aanzshat with an accent *so* royal to the point where it was barely understandable.

# CHAPTER XI

# Maybe we should be businessmen.

All three of us stayed quiet.

"You can speak, children, I won't kill you...until I have to," he declared, ominously.

"What do you want from us?" Kanzon asked, his tone as calm as always.

He pointed at me.

"Me?" I pointed at myself.

"No, not you...but what you have..." he spoke, ominous as ever.

"What do you mean?" I knew he was talking about The First, but I decided to act clueless.

"The First Instrument of Unity!" he yelled, "Are you not aware of the object you possess?"

We didn't reply, but 'Instrument of Unity' – that sounded new. Is that what Seren wanted me to know?

"How can you be—" The emperor was losing his patience, but Senator Shrizas, Daq's mom, interrupted him.

"Your Highness, maybe you could explain what you mean to the children, maybe that could help?" She said in a perfectly calm tone.

"I second that," remarked Senator Aashtus, Daq's dad.

"Third," declared the male general, his voice sounded like freshly made metal.

"Fourth! Yippee!" yelled the female general, her voice quite the opposite of her counterpart.

"Alright," the emperor muttered.

"You," he pointed at me, his voice even more ominous than before, "You hold the first Instrument of Unity. Do you truly not understand the power you possess?"

I didn't answer. I thought I should've said something, but before I could've thought of what to say, he continued.

"Eons ago, before time and space, the Primordial Chaos reigned, an infinite void of everything and nothing,"

The mention of this void of everything and nothing rang some bells in my brain, I felt like I'd been there. Is that the place where I saw Seren when she was in pain?

"In that void were three people – the creators. They sought to bring order to the cosmos, and decided to craft the Apparatus of Unity, a device so powerful that it could unify Gravity with the other three Fundamental Forces," he continued.

The mention of three people confirmed my doubts: I *had* been to the Primordial Chaos – it was the place where I heard the four lines which have been giving me goosebumps ever since I was a little nine-year-old:

*"To unify the universe and bind the deep,*
*To end all entropy or make the cosmos go to sleep,*
*Three artefacts, women of darkness,*
*Three factions, and a power to harness."*

Everything was starting to make sense now. Is this what Seren wanted me to know?

Before I could think further, he continued *again*, "For ages, my ancestors searched for it – Srizure, Dezisk, all of them. A knowledge that many have sought, but none have truly achieved. Even in a distant world Earth, men pursued it. Albert Einstein – you may have heard of him in your intergalactic lessons – spent years of his life striving for a Theory of Everything, unaware of what this knowledge could truly bring. He failed, just like everyone before him and after him...until now..."

All of this sounded insane. There was *no way* that a single device could do so much, and there wasn't *any* way whatsoever that those stupid Earthlings, who think they're the only living things in the universe, could find it. As I thought all this, Aanzshat's tone turned colder and his glow grew stronger, "But three parties – us, the Sosush Empire, Wielders of Quantum Mechanics, the Yazoto Foundation, Masters of Plasma, and lastly, the Trisazal Dominion, Harbingers of Dark Energy – knew better. We knew that the Apparatus was not a mere idea – it was real. With it, we could—"

"Wait," I interrupted him. The mention of the Dominion reminded me of Seren's message: 'The Dominion...they have them. They have The Second and Third. You need to hurry. Reach the Unraveller. *Quick.*'.

"Your Highness, I might know something you don't..." I spoke, my voice trembling with fear.

"And what is that?" he snarled. I could hear and *sense* him getting annoyed.

"You mentioned the Dominion, correct?"

"The Trisazal Dominion, yes. Why?" He was genuinely curious when he asked that. I got his attention.

"Are you aware that they have The Second and Third?"

"*What?* That is *impossible.* That's impossible unless...unless..." his face tensed, "General Ishazust, check the Galactic Status of the Foundation *ASAP.*"

Ishazust pressed some buttons on the part of the armor above his hand and some hologram came up – I couldn't quite comprehend it, but his face told me that it was bad news.

"Your Highness," the general stuttered, "The...the Foundation...they've been overthrown...by..."

"The Dominion," I finished his sentence as he nodded.

"We're done for," the emperor muttered with a sense of disappointment in his voice, like a guy who'd prepared for such threats his entire life and just arrived a day too late, "They will...they will wipe our galactic system...there's nothing we can do now!"

He threw the goblet on his throne ahead of him, shattering it into pieces.

"Uh, your Highness?" Daqpo finally spoke, his voice barely coming out of his throat, "Maybe we can help."

"You're just kids!" he yelled, "You can't help *anything*!"

"Your Highness, we have The First, as you call it, while the Dominion have The Second and Third. Do these Instruments of Unity, as you call them, have any effect while they're separated?"

The emperor didn't reply, he was too busy seething in a mixture of anger and disappointment.

"Not that we know of, no," the female general spoke, "What do you propose?"

"Then we might be your only hope," Kanzon proposed, "My friend right there, Yelix," he pointed at me, "He possesses a power, a power that he doesn't quite understand – a power so destructive, that if under control, it can match the Dominion's Dark Energy."

"This power you speak of...how does it work?" inquired General Ishazust.

"That is *exactly* what we don't know. We were on our way to this place...the Unraveller of Entropy's residence, to *understand* what had been happening in his life recently, but then the pracos attacked and then you took us in!" yelled Daqpo. In front of me, I could see his parents smile at him – they were probably happy with his newfound confidence.

"The Unraveller? But she's a myth! She doesn't ex—" the female general started speaking, but then the emperor cut her sentence.

"How do you know of the Unraveller, child?" the emperor asked, his voice now polite.

"It's a long story, Emperor Aanzshat, we do *not* have the time!" I cried, "Please, let us reach the Unraveller and give *us your* support. If we succeed in first controlling my powers and finding an answer to what our next steps should be, we will give the Apparatus to you. You are *our* emperor, we know that you want what is best for us, and we will help you, even if you sent an annoying Vazhuru to kill us...please, your Highness!"

As soon as I mentioned the Unraveller, I could see a spark in his eye, as if he knew who she was.

"How am I supposed to trust a kid?" he asked.

"Your Highness, you trusted a kid to build about half of your arsenal and then proceeded to backstab that same kid, breaking the promise you had made to him: a promise of peace!" yelled Kanzon.

"Are you...Kanzon the Mechanic?" the emperor inquired.

"Yes!"

"Trusting you boys may be a gamble, but it seems I have little choice...if you do tell the truth, perhaps fate has a hand in this. Very well, General Ishazust, unload them on the coordinates I shall share with you," the emperor commanded.

"Emperor, I can't help but ask: how do you know where the Unraveller lives?" I inquired.

"She taught me how to control Quantum Phenomena."

CHAPTER XII

# I eat pressure for breakfast.

Great. Now my parents, a beautiful girl, *and* an entire empire rely on me. No pressure at all!

As we got ready to leave, I saw the emperor smile for the first time ever, it was like mentioning the Unraveller gave him hope – which I didn't mind, honestly, or else I might've been dead by now.

He gave us some gear as we left, most of which Kanzon said was made by him, but the rest of it was made by the Empire.

Our gear looked something like this:

1.  Quantum Rifle for Kanzon, it was an upgrade on his Plasma Rifle – made by Kanzon,
2.  Three Quantum Shields, made by Kanzon,
3.  One Quantum Sword for Daqpo, the same one that the Vazhuru wielded,
4.  A Quantum Band for me, made by Kanzon,
5.  Six Quantum Repair Kits, made by the Empire.

We were stacked. Before we began our descent from that same glowing thing that we came up in, I could see Daqpo's parents smile at us, whilst the emperor and his generals were pacing around the throne room, hoping that *we*, three sixteen-year-olds, prevent a potentially impending war.

Going down, I felt this new sense of hope, because now I knew someone who had actually *vouched* for the Unraveller's existence and that I wasn't just blindly following whatever Seren had said. As we passed the threshold, I felt the same body-vibrating hum and we went down at a speed faster than what we came up at...but we had a smooth landing, nonetheless.

We reached the ground. In front of me was a small house in the middle of the woods. From the outside, the house was shaded in an oblong color, and there were *no* windows along with no other external details.

The Unraveller really liked hiding...and I couldn't quite understand why. If she was as wise as the emperor made her out to be, doesn't it make sense to give her wisdom to everyone in the universe? Wait no, as I just said that I realized what that'd do – so many bad people as well, but still, why does she *have* to hide?

Anyway, we started approaching the door in the ominous environment of the woods: all the dense and green trees were overgrown, and there was this smell...a smell so disgusting it made my nose burn.

The smell got stronger as we got closer to the house.

"Guys, I have a bad feeling about this," mumbled Daqpo, his voice cracking as he said it.

"I know," I agreed, "But we don't have any other option..."

"Wait," Kanzon said, as we halted to a stop, "Before we walk in, at least get your weapons ready – we do not know what's at the other end of the door."

I hesitated, "Can you at least explain how my thing works?"

"Yeah, same for mine. Like, I know I just need to swing the sword but how do I change its shape...if you get me?" Daq added.

Kanzon started, "Okay, Daqpo – your sword? Get it out."

Daq took the sword out of its sheath.

"Look at the halt," Kanzon continued as Daq followed whatever he said, his sword glowing with the same patterns as HzZ's, giving me serious flashbacks, "There's a button there. The sword's made of quantum-adaptive alloy and makes use of superposition – it can exist in multiple potential states. The button, embedded with a quantum decision core, will trigger a wavefunction collapse, which will essentially force the material to take a specific shape from its potential states, depending on the need at that moment."

Daqpo looked at him, confused, "So I press the thing, and it'll change, right?"

Kanzon grumbled, "Yeah, in layman's language."

He turned his attention to me, "Now, Yelix, your Quantum Band—"

I interrupted him, "Hey, man, in all kindness, don't mention all the advanced physics and just tell me what to do and what will happen in what did you say? Layman's language."

He grunted, clearly frustrated, "Okay. The band, once you put it on, will basically form a neural connection with you—"

"Wha—"

I was going to ask, 'What does neurally mean?', but he cut me, "Shush! It will basically connect with your brain and do whatever you want it to. Additionally, it can make you phase through things as well, for a temporary time period – there's a button for that. Moreover, it can also turn into a grappling hook, and a small blade."

"*Woah,*" I gushed.

"What about the gun?" Daqpo asked.

"I have to use it, you idiot, you don't need to know how it works. Ugh, let's move," Kanzon barked.

"But—"

"You said I'm the brains of the group, right? So, *let's move.*"

Like loyal viziks, we followed him.

We reached the entry.

"EWWWWWWW!" Daqpo grimaced.

"Who wants to open it?" Kanzon asked.

Daq and I didn't answer.

"Fine. I'll do it myself if you losers don't want to help me," Kan muttered.

As he opened the door, Daq and I stepped back a bit and the material made a loud *eeeeeeeeee.* noise.

Kanzon fell to his knees.

"Kan!" Daq and I shrieked.

He didn't answer.

We went straight to him.

"She...she..." he could barely speak so he pointed in front of him.

In front of us, in the middle of the brown walls that the singular room of the house had lay the body of a woman.

The blinking star.

The Unraveller was dead – someone got to her before us. *That* was the source of the smell.

My heart sank. The journey I had set myself on was dangerous as is, but as time passed, it kept getting scarier. I *knew* I should've ignored Seren. The Unraveller was supposed to be a woman with a huge amount of wisdom, heck, she even taught my galactic system's emperor how to control *his* power. How could she be taken down? Or *who* could take her down?

I didn't know what to do anymore.

The Unraveller was supposed to solve all the many questions I had, but with her gone, I was stranded.

What could I say to the emperor, who was then depending on me? What about my parents?

I *needed* Seren. I couldn't understand what to do. Was this my fate? Was all this just for nothing? No, it couldn't have been.

"Kanzon, get up," Daq said while helping him up, "And Yelix, get your head out of your hands."

I hadn't even realized that my head was in my hands. Kan and I listened to Daqpo, who was surprisingly *very* commanding.

"Guys, I know this is a massive setback, but we need to keep hoping. The Unraveller couldn't have just died without leaving *something* behind. Let's investigate."

As if our brains were completely in sync, we immediately went to the body.

I couldn't believe what I saw.

The Unraveller's body lay on the floor, her limbs twisted into different alignments. Her skin wasn't pale yet, meaning that she was killed only recently. Around her wounds were absolutely no bloodstains, which gave me a weird vibe, because instead of them, her body was...twisted, as if space had warped. It looked sort of like the effects of whatever power I had, but destructive – like, my power seemed to warp space together, while this warped space outwards. I don't know if that made sense, but that's the best way I could explain it.

Across the pure black dress she was wearing, I could see spots...spots where space still looked like it was being pulled outward. Whatever energy was used to kill her, some remnants were still around. On her face, her pitch-black eyes were both scarred, and her mouth was open as if she was in the middle of a sentence when she died. Her grey hair was a mess, it looked like it had just been rubbed by a balloon – kind of reminding me of the static electricity chapter I studied in my science class in sixth grade. But behind her hair, I could see something...a note, of sorts which seemed scribbled all over.

"Guys!" I pointed at the note.

"Should we...have a look?" Daq asked.

Mister Practical Kanzon went ahead and took the note, instantly starting to read it.

*"To the Arbiter – If you read this, I am no more. I have watched you grow. Your questions, your doubts, your cluelessness, your fire – it has all been part of your path. Seren, though once silenced by me, holds all the answers you seek. She exists as mere energy, for reasons I do not have the time to write about. She must return, for she is your only hope. In the woods is the key to her freedom – a key that only you can sense, a key that can give her physical form once more after many, many eons. The key produces a resonance that only you can sense, Arbiter. Find it. Free her. Please succeed, for your failure would lead to the failure of the universe. All the best."*

The Dominion had got to her.

# CHAPTER XIII

# Search and don't destroy.

"The Arbiter...who is that?" Daqpo asked, his voice trembling.

"Me," I said.

They both stared at me.

Then I told them about the dream, "Yeah, Seren called me that as well – the Arbiter. That's when she told me about the Dominion collecting The Second and Third as well. Also, guys, come on. I think the mention of Seren made it quite obvious that it's me."

"Well, maybe, I guess, but she could be two-timing you with another guy with mysterious powers," Daqpo quipped.

Kanzon made a weird face, "Not the time for jokes, Daq."

"I'm just saying, man, it's a possibility that this has nothing to do with him and therefore us."

"It does," I said, my tone serious, "We need to free Seren."

"But how?" inquired Daqpo.

"I don't know."

"Great, so we're stranded here with no idea about what to do. Should we just start walking back home?"

"No," Kanzon intervened and then looked at me, "Yelix, her note mentioned a key which only *you* could sense. Can you do me a favor?"

I nodded.

"Use your power."

"But if it activates...you guys might get hurt."

"No. Daqpo mentioned how *only* the Vazhurus were hurt by the activation; the power only hurts those who you *want* to hurt, somehow."

"I guess that's true, but what if it fails?"

"We have no other choice."

I hesitated, "You have a point...I guess."

"Let's make some distance," Daqpo told Kanzon.

And they did exactly that.

As soon as they were at a safe distance, I closed my eyes and clenched my fists. Nothing happened. Honestly? I was getting really tired of this. Like, throughout this whole chain of events, I was only really useful at the start. Since then, it's just been Kanzon with a sprinkle of Daqpo. But that couldn't continue. *I* got them into this. *I* started this.

*I* needed to help out where only *my* power could work. Plus, Seren was involved so that was just extra motivation. We had this...this connection, which I couldn't really understand, but it made me care about her. Plus, she could help fix all my doubts, so there's that as well.

I focused more. I thought to myself, 'C'mon, random stick power, activate!', still, no luck.

I focused even more and thought, 'Seren, help me out, man,' hoping that she'd somehow hear me and just then, I heard this hum...a weird hum coming from the left side of my ear: it was faint, but I could hear it.

I started moving with my eyes closed, "Follow me."

That was probably the most serious I'd ever sounded.

I don't know how I was managing it, but I was able to avoid all the obstacles in the way: door? Perfectly through it. Upcoming tree? Evaded.

I could hear Daqpo and Kanzon mumble stuff like, "He's gone crazy," but I just could not care less. I was focused. This was the first time where I actually felt in control of whatever was inside me.

We made our way through the woods as the sound of what I assumed to be the key got louder, but soon enough, the sound started getting obstructed by this violent sound of water running at riotous rates, as if we were approaching a waterfall or something.

And, well, as always, I was right. I continued moving ahead until I felt someone hold me from behind – it was Daqpo, he yelled, "Yelix! Stop!"

I yelled back, "Why?"

"Open your eyes!"

I opened them.

I immediately took a step back.

In front of me was the massive gap between two ends of land, with a beautiful yet terrifying free flowing river about fifty feet below me. Rivers, on Keo III, looked like a shade of blackish-crimson-red, reflecting the sky above them, so they kind of looked like blood which always gave me the chills – one of the main reasons why I could never be a swimmer.

On the left, there was a continuation of the land we were on, while on the right, there was a terribly powerful waterfall. It was making a sound so loud that, as soon as I got out of power-focus mode, it was deafening.

On the other side of the huge gap, on the land, I could see something shining in a light shade of brown. It *had* to be the key.

"Do you guys see that?" I pointed at it.

"See what?" Kanzon asked.

"The shiny little thing there!"

"Uh, are you having visions?" Daqpo inquired, his voice surprisingly genuine.

"No, there's something that's glowing in a shade of brown...it has to be the key," I murmured.

"Are you sure, Yelix?" Kanzon queried.

I nodded, "Yeah. One hundred per cent sure."

"How are you going to get there, though?" Daqpo asked.

"Kan, you mentioned there was a grappling hook on this thing, right?"

He nodded.

"How do I unlock it?"

"Wear your band and think of grappling hooks," he recommended.

"What the biology?"

"Just do it."

Kan said it, so I did it.

I wore the band on my right wrist. Immediately, I felt this sensation inside of me, a sensation which made me feel like the band was part of me. A sensation that wasn't quite the same as the one that stick gave me, but a strong one, nonetheless.

I pictured a grappling hook in my head, and, as I did it, I could see the band glow and grow – grow in the sense that a grappling hook started forming, a claw-hook extended near my hand, while some buttons formed on the band part of it.

"Woah," I muttered.

"The power of Quantum Mechanics!" Kanzon bubbled, overflowing with excitement.

"Hey, Kan, teach me how to make this stuff sometimes as well, yeah?" Daq asked him, playfulness slowly coming back in his voice.

"If I teach you, you're going to make some superposition food thing, man!" Kanzon joked.

We all laughed. I felt the mood relax for a bit. We had been through so much in the past few hours, so I felt like we all needed some light-hearted time as well. It reminded me that even though things are so tense, I always have my friends, and my family, to look out for me. It felt like hope was revived inside of me.

"So, do I just aim to that side and press the button?" I inquired.

"Yeah," Kanzon confirmed.

Daqpo looked confused, "What if the length is too short?"

"It won't be. I made it, after all."

Daqpo shrugged.

"Alright then, here goes nothing!" I pressed the button.

*FUSHHHHHHHHHHHH.*

A rope extended behind the clawed grappling hook and pulled me with it.

I thought I was about to die because it hadn't yet attached itself to the other end of the massive gap. I was in a freefall state.

Daq and Kan both yelled, "Yelix!"

I tried my best to position the grappling hook towards the edge of the other end as far as I could, but it felt like I didn't have any luck.

I was nearing the river at a precarious speed, and I had given up – but then I felt a sudden surge of energy.

The energy I felt at the Fields.

My dormant powers, whatever they were, were back. I don't know how or why, but they were back, and I literally could not care enough to wonder about the reason.

*BOOM.*

Like a shockwave, as I was about five inches away from the river, I got boosted up.

My grappling hook connected to the other end of the land, and with a breath of relief, I landed safely.

I couldn't believe what had just happened, but there was no time to be shocked. I *had* to materialize Seren as soon as possible.

I yelled at the top of my lungs, hoping to communicate with Daq and Kan, "GUYS! I'M FINE!"

In the distance, I could see them giving me a thumbs-up.

I then turned my attention to what I assumed to be the key. It was right in front of me: a small little object, shaped like an ellipse, seemingly burning with a brown glow.

It had the same little triangular shapes that were on Seren's gown. It *had* to be the key.

Without hesitating, I tried picking it up.

As soon as I came in contact with the key, I felt this spark, a spark that made my finger burn, making me recoil backwards.

The key clearly was meant to be touched by nobody. It was burning hot, and even a second's worth of contact hurt my hand worse than my biology lessons hurt my brain.

But I couldn't give up. I *had* to withstand the pain. There were *so* many people counting on me. I could *not* let them down, not in the right consciousness at least.

I bent over to grab it again.

This time, however, I continued grabbing it. It hurt me, but I couldn't let go. I *had* to keep hold of it. I could *not* let go. I put all my willpower into calming the brown flame down.

I held on, and I could feel it calming down as if I was becoming one with it.

*Fshhh.*

The key stopped glowing for a moment.

I thought I'd finally calmed it down.

Never mind. Nothing can go my way. As soon as I thought that it had calmed down, the object seemed to hop out of my hands, as if it became its own entity, its own entity with a mind.

I quickly made some distance from the object, scared of what it might bring.

Then there it was, in front of me, hopping up and down: Seren was trying to set herself free.

I got up again, thinking that *maybe, maybe* I could do something about the object, maybe I had to throw it to unlock her? Yeah no, that sounded dumb. I still got up though, thinking of methods to unlock her.

But it looked like thinking wasn't required.

As soon as I got up, the object started glowing again – but this time, the glow was different. It was white – white like Seren.

Woah. Honestly, I didn't know what I felt; it was a mixture of awe, relief, and nervousness, mixed with a bit of fear. Before I knew it, the object seemed to crack open, and from inside, I could see the glow growing in size, getting stronger – almost blinding. Usually, I'd be clueless, but this time, I *knew* what was happening. I *knew* that it was Seren setting herself free, so I just stood there and watched, risking myself going blind but the phenomenon was worth it.

From the constantly growing and glowing light, I saw a human shape start to form – it was a human I'd seen before. I knew it was Seren but I waited for the glow to end, excited as heck because this would be the source of my questions being answered...and, well, I'd be lying if I didn't confess that I had developed a small crush on Seren as well.

As I waited, the glow's size and strength reduced, and I could see her.

Seren was here. No more a dream, no more in a massless form of energy. She was her, and she was real.

I pinched myself just to confirm.

# CHAPTER XIV

# Oh, my Math.

Wow. Just...wow.

She was just as beautiful as she was in my dreams. Same clothes, same infectious aura, same beauty. Indescribable.

I couldn't believe she was real. It was just...Math, unbelievable.

I think I was staring because she made a weird face, so I instantly looked away.

But then she mumbled, "How am I...here?" while feeling her arms and the rest of her body, seemingly unable to believe that she wasn't entrapped as a massless entity anymore.

She continued her mumbling, "I can feel...everything...the air, the ground...everything...it's here."

"Is the Unraveller..." she trailed off.

"Yeah," I murmured.

"So, you—"

"Yeah, I still don't have the answers to my questions. I was thinking maybe you could—"

"Yes, I'll do it. First, get me to the Unraveller's place. My home."

"But how do we get—"

Before I could finish, I could hear Kanzon and Daqpo yell, "Yelix!"

I replied back with, "Yeah?"

"Look at this!" yelled Daq.

Daqpo presented a massive wooden log of wood.

"Uh...what is that?"

"Just wait and watch!"

He threw the log of wood and oh my Math. Mid-air, it started expanding, sort of like the Arnazt 7, except it grew much more than it. It was glowing, and somehow, it was also making mechanical noises. Kanzon really, really never fails to surprise me.

"How the heck did Kanzon build that in such less time?"

"I don't know, man, he's a genius!"

In front of me was a half-bridge. Half because it had shortened the distance between the two ends, but it still hadn't connected them.

"We didn't want you to risk dying again! Not with her on your side!" Daqpo hollered.

"It's not perfect," Kanzon admitted, "But it's enough to make the grappling hook work without risking another near-death experience."

See, everything looked good and all – the distance my grappling-hook-band-quantum-thingie-majingie had to cover was much more realistic than the previous time, Seren was now in physical form, and she said she'd give me my answers when we reached the Unraveller's place.

But then there was also an issue: how in the world am I supposed to get Seren across as well?

Oh, Math.

"Uh, Seren?"

"Mhm?"

"I think you'll...uh...have to—"

I turned red, and she probably knew what I was about to say.

She grabbed onto me. Tight. I felt like I was about to get suffocated because her grip was *so* strong.

So, without any hesitation, I pressed the grapple button again.

*FUSHHHHHHHHHHHH.*

The grappling hook got extended and immediately got attached to the near end of the half-bridge. Thank Math I decided to bring Kanzon along, else we probably would've been dead by now.

Before I jumped, she closed her eyes.

While we were in midair, Seren screamed and my heart skipped a beat as she tightened her grip. For a moment, I forgot how to breathe – not because of the absolute pressure she was applying, but I couldn't decide if I was panicking or, well, like a simp, kind of okay with it...I'm pretty sure I got a bit redder as well, but then I started thinking about how we were able to finish each other's sentences, like, how did I know she was going to assume that the Unraveller was dead?

How did she know that I was about to ask her to answer my questions? It was so weird. But I didn't pay any heed to it – did I mention I'm a pathological liar?

When we were at the lowest point of that parabolic path we took, she whispered, "Don't let go," her voice trembling – but I couldn't decide whether it was out of fear or, well, something else entirely. I don't know which I hoped it was. MATH, I HATE FEELINGS.

As soon as we landed, I immediately let go. Not forcefully, but like I slid out of her grip because it was getting a bit *too* awkward.

"You know the path right?" I asked her.

She hesitated, "No...there weren't these many trees when she entrapped me..."

I started walking, "It's okay, just follow me. It's a long walk."

She followed.

My heart was pumping from all the adrenaline, and this was probably the most awkward I'd been in a *while*.

Anyway, we crossed the half-bridge and joined the other two boys, who somehow weren't as shocked to see Seren as I was.

"Let's go back," I said, with a weird tone of confidence that seemed odd, even to me.

Kanzon and Daqpo made confused faces, who clearly also found my confidence a bit jarring.

"Just...just come on," I grumbled.

So, they did while murmuring amongst themselves.

We were about to enter the woods again but then it struck me, I did *not* know the way back. I had my eyes closed when I came, I obviously wouldn't have.

I had reached a predicament. I had two options: either I come out as an idiot in front of Seren, or I get the entire group lost.

I stopped to make a decision.

Seren, who was right beside me, asked, "Why did you stop?"

"Uh, I got a bit...uh, tired – so I thought I'd get some water," I walked over to Kanzon and Daqpo, "Guys, do you have any water?"

Daqpo passed me a bottle.

I decided to take some time to open it because I had another discussion on my mind.

I whispered, "Uh, Kan, do you know the way back?"

"Yeah," he replied.

"Tell me."

"Why?"

"Bro wants to impress Seren," Daq intervened, grinning like a guy from the circus.

I got red.

"Okay, okay," Kanzon composed himself, "Just follow those little marks I made with the heel of my shoe."

He pointed down to show the type of marks he left to me.

I nodded, opened the bottle, and with an exhale of relief, drank it, then headed back to Seren, who was standing there waiting, humming a tune. It didn't really ring a bell, but holy biology, it was beautiful.

"Yoooo!" I yelled as I jumped back, *instantly* regretting it.

"Are we ready to move?" she asked, her voice as otherworldly as always.

"Yep!"

So, we started moving.

As we stepped into the woods, I glanced at Seren. She was humming that same beautiful tune again, and I didn't even know if she realized. Was she anxious? Was I nervous? Math, I hate how much I cared.

# CHAPTER XV

# FINALLY.

We moved through the dense green forest and the crimson-red haze without speaking a word – well, actually, by we I mean Seren and me, because I could hear Daqpo and Kanzon whispering some abhorrent stuff in the background, which I chose to ignore. Along with that were the sounds of the leaves moving past one another and Seren's beautiful humming tune.

Those were *the most* awkward ten minutes of my life. I don't know why Seren chose to move *right* beside me, while I chose to move *right* beside her.

And I despise Daq and Kan for not trying to include me in their conversations.

As soon as we reached, Seren took a few minutes to mourn the Unraveller's body, Daqpo made some ceasea in Kanzon's portable food-maker, while I watched Kanzon tinker a few more things that I couldn't really understand or was too distracted to even give it a try. We decided that we'd all recuperate in front of the house after ten minutes.

So, ten minutes of extreme excitement later, we met outside.

My ears were sore from all the *thuk.* sounds that were produced while Kanzon was working, but I shook it off by twisting my head left and right like a wild vizik drying water off of its body, unaware that, just as I started doing it, Seren came out of the house. As soon as I saw her, I stopped, and my ears kept ringing.

Her face was red from all the crying she did, and she was still wiping tears off her face, I really wanted to do something about it, but I knew I couldn't. Her eyes were still teary, and I absolutely hated it.

Right behind her was Daqpo, running and yelling like a hooligan while somehow simultaneously keeping the tray of ceaseas balanced.

If there was something he could do without any troubles, it's that he could perfectly protect food.

He quickly distributed the ceasea.

Kanzon, Mister Practical, didn't hesitate to start with business, "Seren, what should be our next steps?"

She took a sip of her ceasea, "Hmm—"

I interrupted her, "You're going to answer my questions first, though, right?"

"Yes, Mister Arbiter," she smiled, making me blush. I thought I did a good job hiding it, but Kan and Daq's reactions said otherwise.

"Where do I begin?" she asked.

"Hmm, well, we know about the stuff you referred to as The First, The Second, and The Third – the Instruments of Unity, and what they make up once joined together. Other than that, we know about the parties involved, and what the Apparatus would do if found. So..." I trailed off.

"You know everything except what your strength is."

"Yes," I gulped, I don't even know why, "Also...I was a bit curious—"

"You also wish to know about why I got imprisoned," she perfectly guessed.

"Uh, yeah."

"And how!" Kanzon gushed.

Seren began, "Well, Yelix, remember when I called you 'the Arbiter of Gravity'?"

"Yeah," I replied.

"It's because your powers are based on Dark Matter. In the Primordial Chaos, it was prophesized that when the Instruments stir again, a boy, wielding the power of Dark Matter, will be born to protect the universe from devastation, and to unite all people within it, to protect them from the endless possibilities the theoretical unification of the four fundamental forces might bring. That boy? That boy is you. Your genes are modified in a way that even the Unraveller couldn't understand, and before you ask, 'why me?', trust me, the universe is very random and unpredictable."

Honestly? I couldn't quite understand most of what she said except the 'protect the universe from devastation, and to unite all people within it' line. How in the world was *I* so important? Mostly, I'd have a panic attack about all the new responsibilities I would've had, but now I just wasn't shocked. So much stuff had happened in the past two days that I just wasn't surprised at this kind of stuff.

What I was surprised at, however, was this Dark Matter thing, "What do you mean by Dark Matter?"

She smiled, math, it was infectious, "Dark Matter is like an unseen sticky substance which holds everything together, the invisible framework which gives the galaxies their shape and balance. It's the force that binds everything into balance. Your powers, your strength, it comes from this nature. You can ripple spacetime to create shockwaves, you can bend reality around you and make the world your weapon, and you can even control the gravitational waves that surround you. You can draw chaos into order. It's a force of connection."

I was so confused, and she could see it. So, she simplified it for me.

"You can make your surroundings your weapon."

"Ah!" I finally understood, "Right, but I can't control it..."

I made a disappointed face. The adrenaline died down and it sort of hit me how I was...not enough for whatever important role I had. Usually, I wouldn't care. But now someone had died, and the fate of the universe was resting on my arms. I thought my careless attitude would get me out of this, but it just wasn't working. I imagined what Mom and Dad would say if they got to know that the universe's fate was in their stupid son's hands – I shook the thought away, it wasn't helping. It was gnipleh at best.

I think Seren could see me getting sad.

"Yelix," she kept her hand on my shoulders, just like I had kept mine on hers when she was struggling, sending chills down my spine, "We still have time. I think I can help you out...the Unraveller gave me her wisdom as well – that reminds me, you asked me about *why* she imprisoned me..."

She trailed off.

"It's okay if you don't wish to talk about it," I offered.

"No. I will," she continued, removing her hand from my shoulder, "She was my mentor. She took me in when my parents passed away, *killed* by the Foundation – who were, at that time, the most powerful in the universe. She shared her wisdom with me, she taught me how to control my ageing—"

"How the biology?" Daq interrupted.

"I'll answer that one later, sort of in a hurry, Daqpo," she continued, "But most importantly, she taught me about the Apparatus, and how it should stay hidden, about the many possibilities that this knowledge...but she told me more than I should've known. As soon as I turned sixteen, without saying a word as to *why* she was doing it, she entrapped me...entrapped me into eons worth of nothingness...nothingness until you were born...until I could find a way to talk to you in your dreams...jury's still out about whether she did it to protect me or to shut me up."

She looked sad, clearly, those memories were too traumatic for her, but my impulsive brain could *not* help but ask, "Wait, how old are you?"

Surprisingly, that put a smile on her face, "Appearance and mental age of a sixteen-year-old, with the experience of someone who has been alive for seven billion – which, I have been, with most   of those years having been stuck in that massless form, without ageing."

That kind of made me feel weird for having a crush on her, but, almost as if she could read my mind, she shook her head, a knowing smile tugging at her lips (maybe I was reading too much into it) and directed her attention to Kanzon, "You asked me about *how* she turned me into a massless energy form...she trapped me in a massless quantum state and made that key the quantum anchor – I think you are smart enough to understand the concept."

I clearly wasn't. I hoped Kanzon was, though.

She continued, "It acted as a miniaturized singularity, a point of infinite density in space-time. When I was in that state, my energy state started entangling with Yelix's once he was born, his powers based on Dark Matter amplified those signals and I was able to make contact with him, while for others, I could just observe. It was weird, for sure, but I am grateful that I could do it. Else, I might've still been in that state..."

I couldn't understand any of that, so many fancy terms and, like, what's these people's obsession with all this 'quantum' stuff, man? Like, give it a break! Use some other word, for Math's sake.

Unlike me, however, Kanzon understood all of it, "Wow. Man, I wish I could meet the Unraveller. She sounds so smart."

"She was," Seren affirmed, "Anyway, I think it's time we get back to business. We need to reach the Gate of Panyrc ASAP. It's the gate that connects the universe to the remnants of the Primordial Chaos – it's located in Pezar. We must get there to avoid the destruction of this galactic system by the Dominion."

"How would the Dominion know that The First is with me?" I inquired because it kind of confused me.

"Once you have two of the Instruments, the Third starts glowing, giving heavily energetic pings through spacetime. Tell me, Yelix, have you ever seen The First glow?"

"Yeah, sort of."

"Show it to me."

I opened my bag to show The First to her.

As soon as I opened it, I thought I went blind. The First was glowing brighter than I'd ever seen it.

"Is its luminosity strength equivalent to the strength of the pings?" inquired Kanzon.

"Yes. We do not have much time," Seren said, her voice trembling, "Two days at best, including today."

She looked at me, "Yelix, would you be fine with going through two tiresome days?"

"I mean—"

I was about to say something like 'I'm used to it' to make her think I'm cool but she cut me in between, "You don't have an option," she looked at Kanzon, "Can you build a small inter-planetary traveler in two days?"

"I guess—"

She cut him in between as well, "You have to, you won't have an option. Ask Daqpo to help."

I would be lying if I didn't find this demanding mode a bit attractive, to be honest, and, as I thought that, she continued, "We must leave this planet by tomorrow night. We *need* the Dominion to sense us near the Gate so that they don't destroy this system, *your* home. Kanzon, Daqpo, get to work."

Daqpo and Kanzon nodded their heads in unison and Daq followed Kan as he ran into the house to probably start working.

Seren started walking in the same route we used to go to the waterfall, "And, Arbiter, come with me."

# CHAPTER XVI

# Is this a...?

As soon as we reached the waterfall area, Seren stood at the edge, soaking in the terrifying beauty of the stream below, the woods that surrounded the area, and the violent waterfall.

She just stood there with her white gown getting blown by the heavy wind and her hands stretched from end to end, all whilst humming that same beautiful tune she was humming on our way back here to the waterfall. The scene looked right out of a famous artist's artwork.

She was enjoying the freedom from the Unraveller's entrapment, so I thought I wouldn't disturb her.

Wrong idea.

She called out to me, "Yelix! Come over here!"

I did exactly that. *Now* I understood why my dad barely talked against my mom – talking against women you might potentially sort of maybe (I will not accept it) have feelings for is scary. I ran over and stood right next to her and looked over at the pretty environment.

After around two minutes of just soaking in the beauty, she turned ninety degrees to the right, and I reciprocated.

We locked eyes.

Math, she was beautiful. Her indescribable eyes were looking right into mine, and her dark wavy hair was blowing in every direction possible, making me melt on the inside. Then, she smiled.

I almost fainted off the edge.

And then, she went in for it. A kiss.

She slowly brought her head close to mine and I reciprocated. Her dark red lips were inching closer to mine, my heart beating faster than the speed of light. I couldn't believe what was happening, it was too...too...I don't even know.

However, as she leaned in, her smile shifted into something unreadable. For a moment, I saw a little glint of mischief in her eyes, but it was too late. As always, she surprised me.

Instead of kissing me, she pushed me off the edge.

Mid-air, I felt the ultimate betrayal. I was like, 'I just basically revived you, bro, why would you want to kill me?' and *multiple* other emotions, disappointment for being faked out being one of them.

As I fell, I moved my hands up and down for the first few seconds to try and somehow magically fly. No luck. Then, I just decided to accept my fate. I fell downwards but *again*, just like when I was going to the other side to unlock her key, I felt a surge of energy I'd felt before —

my dormant powers were back, again. With a shockwave, I move upwards at a dangerous force, way more than the last time. I almost felt like I was about to overshoot and go above the edge of the land, ultimately dying if I landed.

But that didn't happen, fortunately. It's like the power knew that this time I wasn't wearing my Quantum Band, like...like, it knew the exact force I would've required to reach back to safety. It was like a...what did Kanzon call it? Ah, yes, a neural connection, but more than that. It had situational awareness and everything. It wasn't just a power, it was instinct; it knew stuff before I did, the power was alive, in a way.

I reached the edge of the cliff and immediately grabbed on and glared at Seren who was standing right above me, grinning menacingly.

"WHY WOULD YOU DO THAT?" I yelled at her.

"Your training has begun, Arbiter," she spoke, her voice practically dripping with amusement, then grinned again, "You'll thank me later."

She winked, I melted.

I groaned and got back up.

"What's next?" I asked.

"Just follow me, Arbiter," she winked and walked off.

I pulled myself up, and saw her hop-skipping in excitement – while she had seven billion years of experience, she was still the same age as me. She was having a crazy amount of fun ruining my life, so I just played along.

"Where are we going?" I yelled at her.

"Dezisk's Hills!"

"Shouldn't we tell the other guys?"

"The house is on the way; we'll do that then!"

And so, we did.

Up next were the best, yet tiresome, few hours of my life. They were *crazy*.

On our way to Dezisk's Hills, she randomly turned around at times and threw rocks and other objects at me, and yelled, "Use your power to deflect them! Also, don't close your eyes, else you'll fall," then proceeded to make that silly tongue-out face.

So, for the first time in my life, I had to use my power without closing my eyes, else, I would either get hit by a bunch of rocks thrown at surprisingly harsh speeds or fall to my death without *any* surety about whether my powers would activate or not.

Honestly? The simp inside me was fine with her endlessly throwing the rocks, but I knew I had to figure out how to use my powers, how to actually be able to hold my own against whatever was waiting for me at Pezar.

So, I locked in.

I tried to search for the power within me, I had this newfound passion, and *finally* after getting hit about seventeen times, I finally was able to deflect one, then two, then three and so on and so forth. I realized I could do this by moving my right shoulder.

Once we got to a plain layer of the hills where a pack of viziks was playing with one another, Seren gave the largest grin possible and ominously said, "Now, it gets harder."

She went over to the viziks and talked in a language that I couldn't really understand, and, before I knew it, one of them left the pack and started chasing me around as she sat there and played with the rest of the pack, laughing with them and then at me.

She said it was for 'durability', but I didn't really understand the point of making such a cute creature become so terrifying.

It endlessly chased me around while I surprisingly kept up until its tail turned from ice to fire, i.e., it got cold, and the evening was here. She yelled out a command to them in that same language she spoke previously and then the vizik stopped chasing me.

She hugged all the viziks and got up, "Let's go!"

"Aren't we going to go back?"

"Nope!"

So, we continued up. We kept moving as she threw projectiles at me while I deflected them until we reached the next plain layer of the hills, where we saw a wild paraskti.

She did the same thing as she did with the viziks and talked to them in the same language that I couldn't understand. Was it the language of the creatures of the Hills? I didn't know.

As I thought that, the paraskti came over and punched me in the face.

"What was that for?" I yelled at her.

"Endurance," she said as she laid down, "Survive ten continuous punches from the paraskti and then I'll ask it to stop. Then, we can sleep."

"Wait, aren't we going back to the house?"

She settled in comfortably on a huge leaf, "Nope. Your friends will come here tomorrow night. You must be prepared by then."

'Okay,' I thought to myself, this shouldn't be very difficult.

"Oh, did I tell you that these creatures are *really* good at physical stuff?" Seren said as she grinned.

"I hate you," I grumbled as I received another punch.

Third, fourth, fifth punch. My face was starting to hurt *really* bad, but I couldn't give up – I wanted to sleep, I wanted to come out as cool in front of that goofy woman, and I wanted to be worthy of my powers, weirdly enough.

Another five punches.

"Done!" I yelled to Seren.

"Well done, Arbiter," she acknowledged, then immediately changed her language to whatever the paraskti understood and asked it to stop and go away, I think.

She gestured at the leaf set about two feet away from her, "You can sleep now. We have your final test tomorrow."

Before I could close my eyes, she muttered, "Tomorrow's going to be unforgettable, Arbiter."

Then, we swapped good-night wishes.

# CHAPTER XVII

# I hate her.

"You talk in your sleep," she mumbled while towering above me, looking at me with a smirky face as I was comfortably sleeping on the huge green leaf.

I rubbed opened my eyes after I heard her say that.

"Get up, it's time we move," she made that moving gesture with her hand and walked off.

Surprisingly, this was the first day in my life when I had a dream that didn't include Seren – it was a general beatdown by the pracos, but I was kind of relieved by that. I really didn't want to get up from my cosy leaf, I was finally able to get some shuteye after two days, and I wasn't done yet. I wanted to sleep more; like, a small nap couldn't have doomed the universe, right? But I had to listen to Seren. She knew more than I did.

"Could've let me sleep for a bit more time," I grumbled as I got up.

She was hopping around in full energy, "Yelix, you were asleep for fifteen hours. I went over to the house to see Daqpo and Kanzon's progress as well. They're almost ready."

"*How?*"

"Your friends are geniuses."

"Daqpo is just a nice dumbhead."

"Okay, your friend, Kanzon, is a genius."

"Mhm."

"Race you to the top!"

"WHAT?"

She started running to the top.

I hesitated, but MATH, her energy was infectious. I accepted her challenge and followed.

Seren was *quick*, because, before I knew it, she was already halfway up whatever remained of the hill we were on. She jumped over fallen trees and swung from branch to branch like a praco.

Me? I couldn't continue straight for more than two steps. Unlike her, I didn't know how to do all the stuff she was doing, and I was barely used to any kind of physical exercise.

To make it worse, Seren yelled back stuff like, "Slowpoke!", "I'll just take a nap while you're falling behind," and other annoying yet adorable stuff like that. There was a part of me which just wanted to not try to beat her, and it kind of gave me validation for not being physically able enough, but the other part was worried about how, if I don't try, Seren's attempt at training me might be a failure.

It took me a few more falls and a few more branches hitting my head to complete weighing the odds. I decided to go with the latter.

I decided to observe how Seren moved – she was swift, almost like she was in a flow state; she knew what to do as soon as she saw the hurdle ahead. She knew when to duck, she knew when to jump, she knew when to move to the right, and when to move to the left. She was amazing.

But then I realized that analyzing her movements wasn't the right idea. There were no set patterns in the environment; everything just came up randomly – I had to fail and see for myself.

*Thwap.* I hit a tree. *Thuck.* I hit a branch. *Vruck.* I tripped.

Slowly but surely, the frequency of the failures was slowing down. Every time I fell, every time I got up, I could see Seren turn around and smile at me. She knew I was trying, and I was glad that it was making her glad – even though it hurt me. Soon enough, the failures just stopped. I realized that I had entered flow state as well. I was extremely proud of myself, and as if Seren could sense me going into flow state, she slowed down a little and let me catch up.

I caught up to her, getting ever so close to the summit, "What happened to the race, woman?"

"You seriously want to do it?"

"Why not?"

I overtook her, but she caught by. We were neck to neck, and I was overfilled with adrenaline – sometimes I was winning, sometimes it was her.

The way to the peak was naturally made like an entrance, four inclined trees were present to welcome us to the peak. Both of us crossed the assumed finish line at roughly the same time, but, in reality, I knew that she won.

However, I was too petty.

"I won," I teased.

"No, I did," Seren crowed, "Also, you might want to look behind you...your final test awaits."

I gulped. When I focused, I sensed a smell which was terrifyingly familiar, a smell which I...a smell of something disgusting.

I turned around, my heart beating out of my chest.

In front of me, looking as disgusting as over, was a praco.

"WHAT?" I yelled as I fell on my butt, probably embarrassing myself in front of her.

"Your final test. Get up, Arbiter. To truly be the Arbiter of Gravity, you must get rid of your fears."

"BUT—"

Before I could finish what, I was saying, the praco charged. I crawled backwards, but it punched me in the face. The back of my head almost hit the ground, but I felt the surge of energy *again*. A shockwave formed from under my head, making the pain almost negligible, causing me to get right up – somehow, on my feet. I finally felt like I was getting a hold of my powers.

I got into a warrior pose – my fists were ready, and my legs were as well. The praco charged again but this time, I was ready. I moved my right shoulder as soon as it got near with three of its arms ready to swing. The praco's hit got deflected away.

I don't know what happened in my brain, but my instincts told me to punch the open air – the result was crazy. The space around me got warped, just like it did in those shockwaves and deflections – but this time, it turned into an arrow of sorts, making it push the praco almost off the cliff. The next thing I did was a kick, it made the same effect as the punch, but this time, the praco got pushed off the cliff. I didn't feel amazing about what I did, but I felt *crazy* good about *how* I did what I did.

I turned around and looked at Seren, "What just happened?"

Seren ran towards me, "You've done it!"

She hugged me extremely tightly, kept her head on my shoulder and squealed, "You've mastered your powers!"

I felt like I was on top of the world, my heart was beating like crazy – I felt the maddest number of emotions that I'd ever felt, whether they were from the fight or her reaction? I didn't know. Seren moved her head to look at me for a second, with the same intensity she looked at it near the waterfall and my heart started beating even quicker. Surely, she couldn't push me off another cliff, right? Either way, I prepared myself for both possibilities. She started leaning in.

But, of course, Daqpo had to ruin it.

From beside me, I heard Daqpo shouting, "Hey lovey-dovey weirdos!"

We both turned our faces to the right.

In front of me was a massive interplanetary travel ship. It was nothing special, with no glow, and no design, but it just had K.D.Y.S. engraved on it. They added Seren's initial. She was now a part of us, that too in *such* little time. Daqpo was standing there in the open door, with the ship hovering in the air with zero sound whatsoever.

Seren looked at me and muttered, "Maybe some other time."

We both ran to the open doors of the ship.

Gate of Panyrc, the Dominion, and whatever else awaited? We were on our way.

# CHAPTER XVIII

# Time to lock in!

The inside of the ship was just as basic as the exterior, which I honestly didn't blame Kanzon for; he barely had any time to make it, let alone design it. The interior was literally just made of one seat for the person controlling the plane, a control center, a couple of windows, some hanging wires, and nothing else.

"Where should we sit?" I inquired to Kanzon, who was comfortably sitting in his command chair.

"I don't know, stand? Or sit on the ground, maybe?" he replied.

His voice was a mixture of tired and annoyed, probably because building something like this was way more than a two-day task.

"Have any of you ever been on an interplanetary trip?"

Daq and I affirmed, but Seren didn't.

"I, uh, never had the opportunity..." she trailed off.

"It's fine, just stay calm and observe the stars as you move past," I assured.

"It's a lot of fun, nothing to worry about," Daqpo added.

Seren nodded, still with a hint of worry on her face.

My brain brained, and a thought hit me.

"Wait, where did you guys even get the materials to make this from?" I asked.

"Kanzon built an undetectable contact device seconds after for me which I used to call my parents, who provided some unsanctioned materials from the Empire," Daqpo responded.

"Woah, you were willing to take that big a risk?"

"Yeah, I mean, we didn't have any other choice."

I couldn't disagree with that, "Fair enough, I guess."

Then, Kanzon yelled, "Guys! We are about to exit Keo III's atmosphere. Prepare for interplanetary travel!"

Daq remained standing, pacing around the ship, observing the beautiful surroundings from the windows. Seren was the opposite – she sat down and stuck herself to an edge and curled up.

"What's wrong?" I went over to her.

"Nothing...it's just...I've never been out of Keo III my entire life..." she replied with her voice trembling.

"It's okay. Come on, get up, look at how beautiful our universe is...look at how beautiful the very thing we're fighting for is." I tried to comfort her.

I offered her my hand. She held it, and I pulled her up and took her to the same window that Daqpo was standing by, and oh my Math. The surroundings were beautiful. Just as beautiful as they were in my previous interplanetary vacations with my parents.

The stars were shining bright, a sight I could barely see on Keo III because of that crazy crimson-red haze and the black clouds. The sight was mesmerizing.

As we moved further away from Keo III, I realized how small it was in comparison to all the other planets that surrounded us, and it made me realize how small I was in this grand cosmic scheme of things. It made me realize that out of all the infinite possibilities of family or groups of friends I could've got, I got the best ones. It made me realize what I was fighting for, and why I had to be prepared for whatever waited for us near the Gate. I had to be ready. This wasn't just for the whole universe – it was for mine.

With that thought in my brain, I continued looking through the window, observing the many fascinating phenomena that happen, or remnants of those that have – such as supernovae. However, as I looked through the windows, the craziest thought came to my mind, a thought that I couldn't believe that I hadn't thought about – what were we even up against?

I looked over to Seren, who was standing to my left, seemingly in a trance because of the beauties of the universe – beauties that didn't really stand anywhere close to her.

I asked, "Seren, what are we up against?"

She gave an innocent laugh, "The Dominion – I thought you knew?"

Daq, who was standing to my right, interjected, "I think he means like..." he looked over to Kanzon, "Yo, Kan, what are the Dominion Harbingers of?"

"Dark Energy!" Kan yelled back.

Daq looked back at Seren, "I think he means to ask about what Dark Energy is and what we can expect from them."

She nodded, "Oh, alright. The Dominion...they're just...they're...they make use of the most destructive scientific phenomena discovered thus far – Dark Energy is essentially the complete opposite of Dark Matter. While Dark Matter binds the universe, Dark Energy – it drives entropy, dissonance, and isolation. Their power thrives on destruction, while yours is the ultimate act of creation. They believe destruction is the route to evolution."

I tilted my head because what in the Math is dissonance?

She got the idea that I didn't understand what she said, "Their strength – it promotes stuff that's not harmonic, it threatens to tear the fabric of existence apart."

That was better.

The Dominion sounded quite scary, to say the least. Why would someone even want to destroy stuff? Like, if your life is bad, why ruin others'? I didn't quite understand.

"Do they have any weaknesses?" inquired Kanzon from the control seat.

Seren shook her head, even though he couldn't see her, "No. They have no weakness – there's a reason why they're the shared-most feared faction in the universe with the Sosush. Only Quantum technology can go head-to-head with Dark Energy technology," she looked at me and smiled, "Plus, what makes our case better is this slowpoke – the only genetically modified being I'm aware of."

Daqpo muttered, "Get a room, guys."

Seren did that awkward laugh, "Anyway – we must remember that the empress will not stop at any cost. We must be ready for anything."

I focused back on the stars, thinking about what awaited us at the Gate but I noticed something out the window...smoke, of sorts.

"Kanzon, what is that?" I pointed at the gas.

"What?" he responded.

"Come here."

"Daq, take control for a second."

Kan left the seat and Daq took his place. Kan rushed over to us and fear took over his face.

He rushed back to the seat, pushing Daq to get off, "Sit down guys, *now*."

"What happened?"

"Alien circumstances – our ship can't handle these conditions. I need to increase the velocity we're travelling at to ensure that the ship doesn't implode. Sit down. Now."

We did what he said. Usually, my heart would've been pounding, the stuff he said sounded scary, but I knew that Kanzon would be able to handle it. Some inner intuition.

He pressed a few buttons on the control console in front of his seat and the ship's speed increased by a tenfold. The thing beamed in front and the view from the windows turned into a blur. Before I knew it, I could feel Seren's cold hand hold my right hand tightly, while on the other side, Daq smirked at me and held the other one as well. Genuinely hate that guy, no joke.

The ship's speed kept getting quicker, and in one of the windows, I could see a nearby planet.

Kanzon yelled, "Entered Pezar's atmosphere!"

We clapped.

Kanzon yelled again, "Engine One has failed! Brace for impact!"

We booed.

The ship tilted and we slid towards Kanzon's seat. Seren's hand was still in mine, and Daq left it and tried to go to the gear bag...and failed.

"Use one of your shockwaves!" he yelled at me.

"WHAT?" I shouted back.

"Just trust me!"

I knew I had control of my power now, but I felt like the ship wouldn't be able to handle the impact from the shockwave...but something inside me told me to trust Daqpo. He was my best friend. Sure, sometimes he might do the most stupid things and sure, he might be the smelliest person on the planet, but I had to trust him.

I let go of Seren's hand and clenched my fists without closing my eyes and a shockwave was produced – he got pushed to the other hand where the gear bag was hanging, and with the tip of his finger, Daqpo grabbed the gear bag, and it fell right towards the control console.

From the corner of my eye, I could see that we were nearing the surface of Pezar. Daqpo opened the gear bag and grabbed all three of the shields and made a protective wall around Seren, himself, and me.

"Kanzon! Get in here!"

Kanzon pressed a few more buttons and tried his best to incline the ship back by around twenty degrees then jumped into the protective wall.

We all held hands and prayed to Math that the landing was successful.

*Brrrrammmmmmmm.*

We landed, and the ship bounced up and down, up and down, up and down at least five times before friction caused it to arrive at a stop. The sound of metal screeching made my ears ring, but at least we were alive.

I pushed the protective wall of shields off just to see that the entire exterior of the ship had crumbled away. All that existed were some parts of the walls and roof, part of the base, and of course, us. Daqpo's spontaneous thinking saved us.

I stepped out of the ship with my back hurting like heck, and the others followed.

Right in front of me, about fifty metres away, in the middle of pure barren land, was one massive black gate shining with a white, otherworldly and ominous glow.

We had arrived at the Gate of Panyrc.

# CHAPTER XIX

# Two's the lucky number!

To be honest, the reveal was underwhelming. I was expecting a *huge*, oversized gate from one of the fictional shows I'd watched. Plus, the planet was also plain boring.

The land was absolutely arid, there were no clouds in the sky – I could see the stars without an issue, something I couldn't really do at Keo III. There was no flora, no fauna, and no humans. All I could see were a few mountains in the distance. Nothing else.

However, as I started to walk, I realized *why* there was no life on this planet.

With every step, I could feel the air getting heavier, making it extremely difficult to breathe to the point where, in just ten steps, I lost all sense of where I was and was about to faint.

"What are you doing?" yelled Seren from behind me.

I turned around, "Going...towards the Gate?"

"Come back here, you idiot, you need to wear a mask on this planet, the air is too heavy to breathe!"

I mocked her, "Damn, okay, you idiot, calm down."

I walked back after recollecting my breath and wore the mask.

Much better. I could finally walk without losing my breath.

I asked, "Let's move?"

"Gear up first," Kanzon commanded.

We used the Quantum gear that the Sosush had provided to us.

Kanzon took his rifle and shield, Daqpo took his sword and shield, whilst I passed my band and shield to Seren.

"Why?" she asked.

"You're not the one who's genetically modified or whatever I am. Trust me," I spoke with confidence which shocked me too.

She nodded, "How does it work?"

I started speaking at the speed of light, "It will basically connect with your brain and do whatever you want it to. Additionally, it can make you phase through things as well, for a temporary time period – there's a button for that. Moreover, it can also turn into a grappling hook, and a small blade," I took a breather, "I quoted Kanzon there, so if you die, blame him not me!"

She smiled.

Kanzon distributed four of the Quantum Repair kits between us and kept two of them back in the gear bag.

Daqpo gulped, "I guess we're ready now."

"Mhm, it's time," I added, "Let's go."

We started moving.

I tried playing it cool – I wanted to act like I felt no pressure, I wanted to act like my heart wasn't beating out of my chest, like my head wasn't about to explode because of all the thoughts in my head.

However, unlike Kanzon and Daqpo, Seren saw through my façade. She hit me with her elbow and talked to me with her indescribable eyes – the message I received was something like, 'Don't be an idiot, you'll be okay'.

That was reassuring enough for the time being.

It took us a bit longer than I expected to reach, but that was because our masks would've stopped working if we walked too fast. Being slow was better than suffocating to death.

The Gate was about five steps away from us when we saw two shadowy figures come from behind it.

They were both wearing menacing, glowing dark purple dresses, purple lipstick, and other types of violet skin makeup that perfectly contrasted their fair skin, with their black hair reaching as far as the middle of their backs. They looked terrifying, terrifying because their facial expressions showed that they probably hadn't smiled in an eternity. All I could see was anger in their eyes.

In their hands were two massive sticks, each of which had a little orb shape at the part that was farthest to the helm.

I was expecting them to charge, but they were just staring at us, or rather, me. Both had locked their eyes with mine and it was getting *extremely* uncomfortable, so, as always, I started yapping, "So are you guys like the...I don't know, guardians of the gate, or something?"

Bad idea.

They pointed their orb sticks at me, and they let out a huge beam of dark purple light at me. I thought I should've jumped away or something, but my intuition told me to rotate my right shoulder to try and deflect it.

My intuitions proved to, shockingly, be correct. Their beam of light didn't get deflected, but I was able to shield myself and the gang. When the bright beam came in contact with the translucent space-rippling deflection wall, I could feel the air in front of me grow denser.

The two forces made a *KH* sound when they came into contact, sounding like some metal object breaking into pieces but backwards. Rather than getting pushed back towards the two scary women, the beam reacted. The edges of the beam started curling, as if it was alive as if it was trying to maneuver its way through the wall. In response, my deflection wall pulsated with a dark hue, rippling outward, fighting back with all its strength.

The point of contact was glowing at a dangerously bright intensity – the contact of black and purple created a beautifully terrifying result. Sparks were slowly beginning to form, and I could feel my defense deteriorating, so I started to rotate my right shoulder at a higher velocity. I know I looked dumb, but I guess it matched my personality.

As I started increasing my rotational velocity, I started seeing more black sparks than purple, showing how my energy was becoming higher than theirs. Soon enough, some of their purple energy got redirected to the sky, some of it started burning the ground, and the rest of it went to either side.

"Give up!" I yelled.

They didn't.

I felt this internal anger coming up from beneath me. From the corner of my eye, I could see Daqpo, Kanzon, and Seren terrified; even with their weapons, they couldn't try to do anything because the sheer contact force my energy with the two women's energy beams wouldn't let them get any angles at trying to use their weapons.

I started getting genuinely pissed off.

I don't know why, but then, out of nowhere, I punched my wall with my left hand, purely out of instinct and I swear to Math that the coolest thing *ever* happened.

The barrier got pushed away towards the two women, taking the two beams of energy with it through an arrow of warped space. They tried fleeing, but it was too late.

The remnants of their own energy hit them in the shoulders, leaving marks similar to what we saw on the Unraveller's body. It seemed like space around that spot had warped outwards with no blood stains whatsoever.

Daq came to hug me, "Dude! That was so cool!"

Kan added, "Looks like your training paid off."

Seren muttered, "You're welcome."

I looked over to her, "Thank you," and then the boys, trying to play it cool, "And yeah I mean it was pretty cool, I guess."

From the corner of my eye, I could see them trying to move towards their orb sticks or whatever they were, which were now about a foot or two away from the Gate, so I quickly ran over to them to kick the sticks away.

"Who are you?" I asked them, my voice sharper than I expected.

One of them spoke, "Empress Koska will see you now."

And then, before I could ask for any more answers, they disappeared with a blinding purple glow.

"What the biology just happened?" I shouted into the thick air.

Everyone stayed quiet for a while, I could still smell the scent of burnt air with that echo of the *KH.* sound ringing in my ear.

Seren broke the silence, "Minions of the Dominion...minions of the empress...she's in the Primordial Chaos."

"So that was Dark Energy? Hm, interesting," muttered Kanzon like a nerd.

"Koska's a cool name though if I do say so myself," muttered Daqpo.

I looked down at my hands which didn't feel like mine anymore. They were unaffected by whatever had just happened, which shocked me because I seriously thought that the impact of the punch would've at least left some after-effects.

The after-effect that did stay, however, was the pain in my right shoulder caused by the constant rotations.

Seren looked at me looking at my hands, "You did well."

Her voice had this calming effect on me, and it made me focus back on reality.

I focused up, "Let's go in."

They all nodded, except Daqpo, who held his finger up.

Daq remarked, "If we go through the Gate, there won't be any going back. Are you all *sure* you're ready?"

Kanzon and Seren nodded.

"No point going back now, else all this would've been for nothing," I spoke with such determination that it even shocked me.

Then, with a deep breath, I opened the Gate.

# CHAPTER XX

# Can stuff stop glowing, please?

Once I crossed the door, I witnessed the polar opposite of what I expected from the Primordial Chaos.

I had been to the Primordial Chaos three times already, and every time, it was the same – everything and nothing mixed into one big dark void where I couldn't do anything.

But this time, it was different. As soon as I entered, I saw this purple glow – a glow I hadn't seen before in the Primordial Chaos but had seen right before entering it.

It was Dark Energy.

The purple glow had surrounded everything, even at a distance.

Right in front of me lay a small device with three rings and a fancy square to lift those rings up. Inside two of the three rings were two objects, objects similar to the First. They had to be the Second and Third. My head went straight away to the Apparatus – because of the three rings, three Instruments and all that, but then wasn't the Apparatus an object on its own? Weren't the Instruments just the Apparatus divided into three? I had to ask Seren.

"What's that?" I asked her.

She shook her head in disappointment as if she thought that I'd have somehow known what it was, "That's a device that the Foundation made to wield the Instruments because of them deteriorating over time."

I gave a reaction which I felt was quite underwhelming, "Oh, crazy."

Daqpo grew restless, "Wasn't Empress Koska or whatever her—"

Of course, he jinxed it.

From the distance, I could see a shadow come out. A tall, feminine shadow – feminine because of the way she was walking. She came out of the shadows, and I could not believe what I was seeing – it was like she was wearing the exact same clothes as Seren, but just in a purple shade along with a couple of bits of armor.

Then her face – she looked *terrifying*, terrifying but also beautiful, like...like a celestial nightmare brought to life. Her features were sharp and angular as if her face was cut from obsidian with her face pulsating in a purple shade, and her eyes looked like two burning purple flames. Her stare was terrifying, and it seemed like she was seeing through every single thought I'd have had in the past. I could only see her hair because of the purple streaks, else the rest was camouflaged with the void.

The armor on her was sleek, yet it gave off a weird hum, dissimilar to most of the other hums I'd ever heard.

She wasn't a person – she was the embodiment of the chaos around us.

She was the empress.

Koska.

Beside me, I could see Daqpo gasp, while Seren tried staring her down.

Kanzon didn't really have a reaction because he was way too busy trying to find the source of the purple glow.

The empress finally broke the silence, "The Arbiter…"

I tried to act tough, "Yep, yep, yep?"

Seren gave me a look that said something like, 'You sure you want to say that?'.

"I've been waiting for this…" the empress continued.

Daqpo tried to join in, "You literally sound like every supervillain in every piece of fiction that I have *ever* watched. Get original."

She clearly got pissed off. She moved her right arm up and aimed it *right* at Daqpo. I knew something she was about to do something. I rotated my shoulders again, trying to make the protective wall again. No luck.

I gulped, "What the biology?"

"What happened?" Seren inquired.

"My powers...they, they...didn't work..."

Right then, a purple light – similar to the one from the orb sticks her minions used – went right towards Daqpo. He immediately put up his shield, but it didn't do much. The sheer power of the beam of light destabilized his grip on the shield, making him fall to the ground.

I'd had enough of her.

I started speaking with a dormant, ready to explode, anger, "Hurt me all you want, but hurting my friends is a boundary that you *cannot* cross."

I did the punching thing this time. From past experience, I ideally would've created a big arrow-like thing warping through spacetime, pushing the enemy away.

But no luck. Nothing happened.

I felt the surge of energy in my body but somehow, someway, the result just didn't come in physical form.

I looked at my hands, "Why...?"

"Feeling useless, Arbiter?" the empress snarked in an ominous tone, slowly making her way here.

I looked over to Seren, who was standing there in shock, "Why are my powers not working?"

She stuttered, "I...I don't know."

Kanzon yelled over to me, "Yelix! Try your best to slow her down!"

He then exited the Primordial Chaos. I wasn't sure about why he did that, but I figured that trusting him was our only option, so I did what he said.

From behind me, Daqpo charged.

He ran with his sword now in the form of an axe. He went over to her and tried to strike. No luck.

The empress held the axe with her left hand before Daq could strike, "Quantum weaponry...hmmm, the Sosush..."

As she said that, I saw a violet shield start forming on her right hand. It was glowing as it grew in size while its hexagonal shape's edges got sharper.

"Daq!" I yelled.

"What?" he yelled back.

Too late. Before I could say anything, she broke Daqpo's axe in half, creating an explosion so huge that it sent Daq backwards yet again.

He looked as if he was in pain – he had to be, that explosion was loud, bright, and *huge*.

"How are you doing that?" I shouted at the empress.

She replied, "Oh, did you think that you were the only one with genetic modifications?"

I stared at her in genuine disbelief – I thought I was the only one with genetic modification, that's what the prophecy said, at least but nope.

"How...?"
"Science has evolved, Arbiter," she was about three feet away now, "Give me the First and I'll spare you and your puny friends."

I looked at Seren. I really, really wanted to take the offer, but I knew that if Koska got control of the Apparatus...the whole universe is doomed – they think the universe will evolve if destruction happens. That is not the way. Seren's face gave the same sentiment. She looked determined, angry even, and she wanted us to never back down, never give up.

"Nah," I clenched my fists hoping for the energy to come out, but nope. No luck yet again.

"For Math's sake!" I yelled in frustration.

As I yelled, Seren charged Koska from beside me, with my, sorry, her Quantum Band glowing in a shade of blue, something that didn't happen when I used it. She pressed the band as she got close to the empress and *boom.* a big shockwave got produced and the empress got pushed back and fell on her butt.

Like a little cheerleader, I yelled, "Heck yeah!"

The empress got back up without much of an issue and tried provoking Seren, "So...the entrapped mentee of the Unraveller..."

Seren had this new angry mode that I'd never seen before, "You have *no* right to say her name, Koska!"

She pressed her band again, creating yet another shockwave – louder than the previous one.

This time, however, the empress was prepared – she made a deflection wall similar to mine by putting up both of her hands. The impact was a beautiful mixture of blue and purple, and it was like the shockwave just disappeared in no time.

The empress started becoming even more annoying, "Oh, I can talk about her. I can talk about *whoever* I killed."

I could sense Seren getting angry, she went in for another strike – this time, her band had turned into a small blade, a dagger of sorts, whilst I could see another purple weapon forming on the empress' right hand – a sword.

They met head-on again – Seren's small blade and Empress Koska's sword, sparking every time they hit each other, warping reality in the process, making spacetime stretch outward. I felt useless, to be honest, because Seren was fighting my fight, it was supposed to be the Arbiter going head-to-head against the empress, not his mentor, friend, or...yeah, no, too soon.

Then I noticed something while being a bystander in their battle – the empress wasn't using her left hand in the fight, instead, she was preparing it for something else – I could see small glows of purple light from the distance.

She was going to use her Dark Energy beam or whatever head-on against Seren.

"Seren!" I yelled.

Too late. The beam had fully materialized. In just one second, Seren would've been in the same state as her mentor. I felt fully useless. I closed my eyes. I didn't want to see her die. I could feel my heartbeat become slower.

I was prepared to hear a shriek from Seren, but instead, I heard a shriek from the empress, "What?"

I opened my eyes. The purple light in the void wasn't there and the empress was not head-on against Seren anymore. Instead, she lay on the ground about five feet away from her, while Seren was standing static. She turned around, her face just as confused as mine.

The confusion had a short stay, though, because from beside me, I saw Kanzon come out, "Sorry it took me so long, guys, had to tinker this thing up."

In his hand was a little metal fork of sorts.

"What is that?" I inquired.

"Well, I noticed that the purple glow was the same as the purple glow on those two ladies outside that we beat – it was Dark Energy, and I figured that, since Seren said that Dark Energy was the opposite of Dark Matter, I realized that the reason why your powers weren't working was the glowing thing that empress had made. I used this little baby here—" he pointed at the fork, "—to reduce the intensity of the zone around you, making your powers work again."

"Wait so did I—"

"Yeah, your powers pushed the empress away just now. Something, or someone—" he looked at Seren, "—made the powers unlock, and I was there on time to make them work."

I hugged him, and Daq, who had seemingly recovered from that massive blow from before, came from behind, "Kanzon, you absolute genius!"

Kanzon commanded me next, "Now keep this fork with you and beat the biology out of her."

Our celebrations got cut short, however, as Seren came over, "Thank you, Yelix, Kanzon, but we have more pressing matters to attend to."

She pointed at the holder for the Instruments, which had now fallen due to the misdirection of the purple beam, with one of the Instruments having seemingly cracked, making stuff around it go haywire.

"The Second – the Strong Nuclear Force Instrument – has broken."

# CHAPTER XXI

# The battle.

In front of me, I could see the empress slowly getting up.

Daqpo asked, "What should the plan be?"

Seren took charge, trying to stabilize her voice, "Kanzon and I will try to handle the broken instrument. You and Yelix, you guys work on defeating us and defeating her."

The three of us nodded.

I asked Kan to hand me over the fork, while Daq asked him for his Quantum Rifle – Kan reluctantly gave it to him. Seren asked for the First so I just gave her my bag.

We walked towards the empress while they got to work, trying to fix the broken Instrument.

My heart was pounding as I saw the empress get back to her normal state as if she wasn't hit by a quantum shockwave, a dark matter shockwave, and whatever else. I was nervous, and I didn't know if I was ready.

But then a voice behind me spoke.

"Hey, idiot!" Seren yelled, making me turn my head, "You've got this."

"Hey, now! What about me?" whined Daq.

"Yeah, you too, Daqpo!"

That was enough to give me the confidence I needed. She somehow knew I needed it, and then Daq's funny intervention reminded me, for the tenth time or something, about what I am in this for. I'm not in this for the universe. I'm in this for mine: my family and my friends.

I kept my hand on Daq's back, "You ready, smelly foodie?"

"Mhm," he affirmed.

"I go short range, you go long. Try not to shoot me."

He nodded.

I charged.

And so did she.

We both produced a shockwave, both of which cancelled each other out in a massive glow of black and purple. My adrenaline was at an all-time high, so the next thing I did was move my right shoulder to create a deflection barrier and push it with a punch, just like I did against two of her minions. She destroyed the barrier with her purple glow of energy. Seren and Kanzon were right — her powers are the *complete* opposite of mine. While my deflections were based on pushing reality together, hers were based on pulling it apart. I couldn't beat her alone, and she couldn't beat me alone. I had the advantage because of

Daqpo.

I don't know why, instincts, I guess, but I created a barrier around myself by twisting my right foot. As soon as the barrier got created and she started shooting her purple beam at it, I yelled out Daq's name and he began shooting – properly this time, to avoid overheating his gun like he did back when we met the pracos in the Hills. None of his shots hit, but it was enough to distract the empress.

Just as she diverted her attention to Daqpo, I kicked reality and sent in another one of my reality-joining arrows at her.

Direct hit.

But her beam of purple light hit Daqpo on his right leg. He fell to his knees.

"Daq!" yelled Kanzon and I in sync.

"I'm fine! I'm fine!" he said as he used his Quantum Repair Kit on the wound, "Focus on the Instrument and that Math-forsaken woman!"

"But—" I tried to say something.

"Just do it!"

So, we did. Kanzon focused back on working on the Instrument with Seren, while I focused on Empress Koska, who was now back to normal.

I was starting to get frustrated, "When will you give up?"

She just laughed.

After she was done with her laughter session, she did something I hadn't really seen before.

She started rotating in one spot and started to make a loud, massive storm of sorts, with purple lines moving all across it, just like the purple streaks in her pitch-black hair. With a big kick, she sent it right towards me.

For a moment, I was clueless. I thought this was it, I didn't think that I had a response for this but my instincts got a hold of me again, I jumped and landed just as the storm got into close proximity, warping space all around me – creating a storm of my own.

My storm looked like it pushed inwards, whilst hers was pushing outwards. Mine was black, hers was purple.

It was a clash of harmony vs chaos, or entropy, as Seren said.

The impact was *insane*, and it lasted for a good fifteen seconds – there was a mixture of black and purple sparks, a loud zzzzzzzzzz. sound, and a large outwards force of wind, which I didn't think could exist in the Primordial Chaos.

 Harmony versus chaos. It felt like a fight that was as old as time itself.

They ended up cancelling each other out and pushed both, the empress and me backwards. I crashed right into Daq, who let out a huge, "Ow!"

"Sorry!"

"No, no, it's okay."

"Are you better now?"

"Yeah, yeah. Now listen, I have a plan, I don't know if this will work or not, but it's worth a try. I'm useless sitting here anyway."

So, he told me his plan. It sounded promising, but I was scared about it not working, "You sure?"

"No, but nothing wrong in trying."

I couldn't disagree.

He gave me his gun and some spare rope and crawled over to Kanzon and Seren; his legs were clearly still in pain, but he didn't want to accept it.

"Just you and me now," I yelled out to Koska.

She laughed.

Math, what was her issue? Was entropy *such* an important goal?
I knew that short range was my only option. Long range wouldn't yield any results whatsoever, it'd turn into a battle

for eternity – and I didn't want to waste my life in an empty void.

I tied the gun to my back with the rope that Daqpo gave me and charged.

I was ready to throw hands.

I did the arrow-punch in an attempt to push her, but her right hand formed a small shield and protected her. Then, her left hand formed a hammer and tried to strike me, but I did the right foot thing and created a barrier to protect myself. We went back and forth for a while, each contact making many *TH. PH.* sounds. I had to somehow push her away...

But then it hit me: why fight with your hands when you have a strong tongue?

I pushed myself away a bit and just started dissing her. She seemed like she had a huge, fragile ego, so I had to try.

"Hey, ugly!"

She looked around.

"I'm talking to you, Princess Purple!"

"How dare you..."

My assumption was right – her ego was fragile.

"Oh, did someone's ego get hurt? Wain-wain-wain, cry to someone else!" I laughed, even though I was dying internally.

"You little!"

She attacked me with her purple beam of light, but I defended it with the right foot-twisting barrier.

"Hahahaha! Your puny little attacks don't work either! Get better. I've seen pracos fight better than this!"

I felt like she was about to explode, but I had to do it.

She shrieked, making multiple throwable purple weapons in her hands and throwing them at me, "Die!"

I jumped, dodged, and deflected all the throwables. 'Thanks for the training, Seren,' I thought to myself.

"I don't die to uglies."

Just as I said that, she charged – weapons in both her hands, just as I expected. A sword, and a five-pronged object.

While she was charging, I implemented Daqpo's plan. I took the Quantum Rifle out of the rope while simultaneously rotating my right shoulder.

I threw the rifle right at the empress, who, without thinking struck her sword right through it, causing a large *BOOM.*, throwing her backwards. I then arrow-punched my barrier right into her body which was now mid-air.

Direct contact.

She fell down, back first.

I ran over to her to deliver the final hit. Daqpo's plan had worked – Quantum plus Dark Matter was what was required.

"Told you, I don't die to uglies."

Then, I arrow-kicked her face. She hit the ground, and didn't get up. It was over. At last.

I looked at her lifeless form and finally breathed a breath of relief. My chest was starting to move a bit slowly, but it didn't last long. But obviously, I could never get a win.

Behind me, I heard Seren's voice cut through the silence, yelling, "Yelix!"

Her voice was trembling with urgency.

# CHAPTER XXII

# Idiot.

I ran right over to her, curious about why she sounded so scared because the state of and around the Instruments was the same as before – stuff was going haywire around one of the broken Instruments.

"What's wrong?" I asked out of utter confusion.

Kanzon replied, "We can't do anything, not before everything goes haywire and falls apart completely."

"What do you mean?"

Seren started, her voice trembling, "The Instruments...they were all—" she took a deep breath to stabilize herself, "—they were all meant to either stay apart or together...but...but the one measure to be taken was..."

Her voice died, so Kanzon continued, "The one measure to be taken was that it could never be broken. Now, with the Second having broken, we need a bridge."

Daq intervened, "Can't we just repair the Instrument?"

Seren started speaking again, her voice trembling more than usual, "We don't have time, we—"

I thought my brain brained, "Wait, Seren, you said my powers are about, like, joining stuff, right?"

"Yes."

"Can't I simply just use my powers to join them together?"

"Do you want to stay in the void forever?"

Oh, for Math's sake, why does everything have to have a catch?

"Okay...what do you mean by a bridge, then?"

"One of us will have to act as the device that the Foundation built and wield the Instruments, completing the Apparatus and granting them all the wisdom in the world—"

"Oh, that doesn't sound like an issue, then. Kanzon? Step right forward and get all the knowledge in the world!"

Seren was starting to get annoyed, "Let me continue what I'm saying," this was unlike her, "We don't know what the aftereffects may be – we must remember that we were supposed to wield an object – the Apparatus. The Apparatus was safe, but this? A bridge? It might not be. That's why I will act as the bridge."

"Are you out of your mind?"

"We have no other option!"

"I'm the Arbiter, I'm supposed to do it."

"You were just supposed to defeat the empress. The prophecy is over. This is all unprecedented."

"But I will do it."

She held her head, "Shut up!"

Daq, "Oooh, a couple's quarrel! Let's, uh, back away, Kan."

I then gave them a side-eye as they backed away.

Then, I calmed myself down because hurting her was the last thing I wanted to do.

"Seren, please, let me do it."

"No," she was starting to tear up, "I can't!"

"Why? I might be able to handle it with my power, you might not."

"That doesn't matter! We're talking about gaining the knowledge to understand how to unify the three entire fundamental forces with the last one, wisdom that no one yet has been able to have...the wisdom that you might get..." she trailed off.

I kept my hand on her shoulder, trying to calm her down, "Continue."

"It might be too much for our brains to handle...we might..."

She started crying.

"We might forget everything, we might forget each other."

"What?"

"Yes."

"It's okay, my brain's quite huge, I'll take the risk."

"It doesn't matter if your brain is huge."

"Well, I have those...what do you call them? The neural connections with my powers. I have better odds."

"Doesn't matter. I'm doing it. Unlike you, I don't have a family, I don't have friends, I just...I just have you."

I froze as I heard that. It was weird, but also real. Weird because we'd barely known each other, real because it was miraculously true.

'I just have you' – that phrase weighed on me more than any kind of force the universe could put on me.

I tried keeping my voice steady, "You have more than just me...you have Daq, Kan, everyone we're fighting for. Let me do it, please."

"No! If you do it, you'll forget all your powers as well!"

"So what? I served my purpose!"

"What if some other threats come?"

"Some other people can get genetically modified; I don't know but *I* am the clear choice to do this."

"You're the future, I'm just—"

"Don't you dare say you're anything, you're more than that," my voice rose, "You've always been my anchor."

I could see that she was starting to get convinced, because a weak laugh escaped her lips, "Why do you have to be such an idiot?"

"I learnt from the best," I said, trying to lighten the mood.

Then, before I could say another word, she took her and my masks off, held my face and kissed me.

It wasn't gentle or soft. It was raw and desperate, filled with everything she couldn't get herself to say. Her lips trembled against mine, and I could feel her warm tears against my cheeks. I would've melted if the weight of the situation wasn't like this, but I just went static.

From the back, I could hear Daq say, "Awwwww."

I would've usually yelled at him, but I couldn't get myself to.

As Seren pulled back, she kept my face in her hands, her eyes locking with mine.

"I love you," she whispered.

But before I could say "I love you too", she let my face go and pressed her quantum band. It glowed blue and let out a shockwave, knocking me into Daqpo and Kanzon.

"Seren! No!" I yelled, but it was too late.

She took the First out of my bag with her right hand and held the Third along with the broken parts of the Second.

I could feel tears going down my eyes as I saw a blinding glow – a glow that made Seren look even more beautiful than she already was. As the glow kept getting stronger, I felt my heart pound faster, terrified of the possibility of her forgetting everything.

As the glow died, I saw Seren fall.

I ran over to her, trying to shake her awake. No luck.

I thought about using the Quantum Repair Kit, but she didn't have any visual signs of damage, rendering it useless.

"Someone get some water!" I yelled at Kanzon and Daqpo.

Mister Logic Kanzon calmly said, "It's better if we leave the void first."

Daqpo nodded to agree.

I hesitated, "But what if she—"

"She won't," Daqpo assured.

I picked Seren, who was shockingly light, up and exited the Primordial Chaos using the Gate of Panyrc, hoping to never see it again.

As soon as we got out, I kept her on the arid ground of Pezar and yelled her name, pleading her to get up as Kanzon ran to get water.

No luck.

Daq knelt beside me, his careless face turning into one of worry. Kanzon ran over with a vial of water which he might've got from some random hidden component of the ship. He handed it to me without a word.

I poured some over her eyes, her lips, and even her nose. My hands were trembling.

No luck. Her face was as still as the stars above. My heart sank.

Then, her eyes fluttered open.

I exhaled with more relief than I had ever done before, "Seren!"

I looked at her eyes – they were...different, they weren't indescribable as I remembered them. Sure, they were still the most beautiful I'd ever seen, but I could find a word for them – they looked like a kaleidoscope, glimmering in too many colors to name.

Her gaze locked onto mine, but I couldn't sense any recognition, "Who...?"

I cried, "It's me! It's Yelix, you know, the Arbiter of Gravity?"

She tilted her head, looking confused but adorable at the same time, "Yelix...an entity of gravity...curious."

I was shocked, "Seren! It's...it's me..."

She blinked, her expression stuck in a poker face, "Keo III...Gate of Panyrc...fragmented reality...scattered across strings..."

Daq asked, "What strings?"

Rather than responding, Seren sat up, her movements mechanical and looked at the cloudless horizon. The air started glowing, shimmering, even, and the barren land of Pezar shifted into colors – blue, violet, green. Cracks started forming as if the sky had turned to glass, pulsing with bright light,

Kanzon took a cautious yet curious step, his voice filled with a weird, scientific curiosity, "Quantum tunneling...on a macro scale? It's...it's not supposed to—"

"Supposed to," Seren cut him, her voice resonating with something ancient, "Supposition is the root of order...but the strings...the strings are infinite."

I grabbed her shoulders out of desperation and shook her violently, my tears providing water that Pezar so dearly missed, "Seren! Come out of this...this trance!"

For a moment, her eyes caught mine and I saw the Seren I knew – the one who laughed, the one who teased me endlessly, whose idiot I was, my anchor, my mentor, the one I loved.

But then, she gave me a bittersweet smile, "Yelix," her tone seemed apologetic, "The strings hum in harmony, but their song is infinite."

And then, was gone. Gone in a beautiful yet weirdly gore way. Her body seemingly unraveled, merging into the threads of light, merging into the cracks of reality. The world around us flickered, shimmering in flabbergasting ways, all the colors growing brighter than before, until nothing.

With a small *peeeesh.* sound, there was nothing.

Just emptiness and silence.

The weight of what I'd lost hit me while Kanzon and Daqpo stayed static, their faces pale.

I fell to my knees, tears dripping down my cheeks.

But then I heard it. From the silence, her hum. The beautiful song she hummed every time she walked, giving me shivers down my spine.

And I knew she wasn't truly gone.

Not yet.

# Key Terms

You can look up the following terms on the internet to further understand the physics that Yelix couldn't, and possibly unlock your inner Kanzon (note: do *not* become like Daqpo).

1. Dark Matter
    2. Dark Energy
    3. Plasma
    4. Quantum Mechanics
    5. Quantum Superposition
    6. Quantum Tunneling
    7. String Theory
    8. Supposition

# Shoutouts To The Real Ones

1. My family (Dadu, Dadi, Nanu, Nani, Dad, Mom, Khushi, Les Australians, Za Delhiites, Los Ex-Dubaians, The Noidans, and The Brits)
2. My weird friends (In alphabetical order because I didn't want to hurt any sentiments (sorry if I missed any of you): Aditya Singla, Anmol Dhingra, Angad Brar, Arjun Mann, Arnav Garg, Arnav Gupta, Ayaan Chotani, Daksh Arora, Devik Ahuja, Gnanav Nand Jagdish Easwar, Harry Choudhary, Ishan Agrawal, Ishant Singh Rawat, Kanan Gandhi, Keyur Kumar Chalavadi Dasari, Khoushil Jain, Kosuke Yoshioka, Neelesh Goyal, Pavaki Kumar, Pranav Chawla, Ranveer Hooda, Rishit Saini, Sksham Mittal, Srijan Seshadri, Suvan Handa, Trishaan Chaturvedi, Upraj Singh Padam, Vaanya Rai, Yashodhan Pugalia)
3. My teachers (Too many to name, I'm in 11th grade, please excuse me.)